NEW LIFE, NEW LAND

By

USA Today Bestselling Author

ROBERTA KAGAN

Book Three in The Eidel's Story Series

CONTACT ME

I love hearing from readers, so feel free to drop me an email telling me your thoughts about the book or series.

Email: roberta@robertakagan.com

Please sign up for my mailing list, and you will receive Free short stories including an USA Today award-winning novella as my gift to you!!!!! To sign up...

Check out my website http://www.robertakagan.com.

Come and like my Facebook page!

https://www.facebook.com/roberta.kagan.9

Join my book club

https://www.facebook.com/groups/1494285400798292/?ref=br_rs

Follow me on BookBub to receive automatic emails whenever I am offering a special price, a freebie, a giveaway, or a new release. Just click the link below, then click follow button to the right of my name. Thank you so much for your interest in my work.

https://www.bookbub.com/authors/roberta-kagan.

DISCLAIMER

This is a work of fiction. Names, characters, businesses, places, events, and incidents are either the products of the author's imagination or used in a fictitious manner. Any resemblance to actual persons, living or dead, or actual events are purely coincidental.

TABLE OF CONTENTS

CHAPTER ONE

The United States of America

Chicago, Illinois

Spring of 1959

Dovid Levi wiped down the counter at the bar where he worked as a bartender/ manager. It was a tavern located on 31st and State Street called Arnie's Little Slice 'O Heaven. He sang softly to himself as he looked in the corner at the small stage that rose up from the sawdust-covered linoleum floor. He stood on wooden pallets lined up behind the bar. He worked long hours standing on his feet, and the linoleum was hard on his knees and ankles. The wood of the pallets gave way with his weight, making it easier for him to stand for extended lengths of time. If one were to get down on the floor and look closely, one could see where quarters, nickels, dimes, and pennies had fallen between the wooden slats of the pallets.

"Must be a fortune in there," one of the beer delivery boys said as he looked at the change between the wooden slats.

"A fortune?" Dovid laughed. "Maybe a few hundred dollars. But we'd have to close for a week and get a child with tiny hands to dig it out."

Dovid kept his bar spit-shined clean. His boss, Arnie Glassman, the owner of the tavern, hated it when the countertop was sticky. He was a perfectionist and if Dovid didn't have a chance to clean the bar, Arnie would nag Dovid's friend and co-worker, Crawford B. Dell, known to everyone as Cool Breeze, to "Get that bar clean."

Cool Breeze had been hired by Arnie as a cleaning man. However, as things turned out, he had a wonderful knack for fixing things. As soon as Arnie learned that Cool Breeze was a handyman, he expected him to fix anything needing fixing in addition to his cleaning duties. Dovid knew that Arnie didn't pay Cool Breeze any extra for his additional work. Dovid had mentioned it to Arnie but Arnie just shrugged his shoulders and said he saw no reason to give the colored cleaning man a raise.

"I pay him enough," Arnie said.

Dovid didn't agree with Arnie, but he was only an employee and had to adhere to his boss's wishes. So, whenever Cool Breeze was busy doing the plumbing or electrical work, Dovid tried to do some of the cleaning to help make things easier on Cool Breeze. That afternoon, as Dovid was straightening his bar, Cool Breeze was trying to fix a broken radio. Arnie was sitting at the bar watching Cool Breeze carefully remove the parts from inside the radio case.

"He has golden hands, that Cool Breeze," Arnie Glassman said to Dovid. "But he can be so lazy." Glassman knew that Cool Breeze was standing close enough to hear him.

"That Glassman," Cool Breeze said and shook his head. He was speaking to Dovid but he was looking straight at Glassman. "He be a slave driver." It was obvious that Cool Breeze was not afraid of losing his job. "If'in you sees me

9

fighten with a bear, Glassman, don't help me, help the bear," Cool Breeze said, glaring at Glassman, who burst out laughing.

Then, within a few minutes, all three men were laughing so hard that Cool Breeze had to put the tiny radio parts down on the bar until he could catch his breath.

Dovid liked the banter between them. His boss was a kind man with a big heart. However, he didn't respect colored people and that bothered Dovid. Dovid enjoyed working with his dark-skinned friend who had an amazing wit and a crazy good sense of humor. As they became better friends, Dovid affectionately nicknamed Cool Breeze "the street philosopher." The two formed a friendship right away on the day Dovid started working at the tavern. Cool Breeze had shown Dovid the ropes, introduced him to the customers and other employees. That first day, after Dovid had finished his shift, he and Glassman had sat down at the bar to have a beer.

"Listen, Dovid, before I go off and hire you on a whim because you're a Jew like me and I feel sorry for you, I know how hard it is to be a yid and get a job in this city. But I have to tell you that bartending in a colored neighborhood is a dangerous job," Glassman warned Dovid. "This is a bar where the colored folks can come and unwind. But you and me, we stick out here, if you know what I mean. Now I have to say that most of our customers are pretty good and they won't give you any problems. But some of them are drug addicts, some have been in jail, they all know you have cash because we work in a cash-only business. And they might need that cash for drugs, if you know what I mean. So, you gotta watch your back all the time. The colored people are different than us; they're a different breed. It's not that I don't like them. It's just that I've been around them and they aren't the same as whites. I don't know if you know anything about heroin? But a lot of these people in here are users, especially the musicians who come in. It's a sad situation because it was the white man who got them started on it. But you're gonna find that smack can drive a man to do things he wouldn't normally do in order to get a fix. What I am trying to say is that when you work here you'll need to carry a gun because you could easily get robbed. If you take this job you better be prepared to see plenty of knife fights break out in here. Gunfights too," Glassman said, biting his lip.

Glassman looked straight into Dovid's eyes. Dovid just nodded his head. He needed work. He still had a little money left from what he'd saved, but he didn't want to spend it without knowing that more would be coming in. He had a wife to support and he took his responsibility seriously.

Dovid shrugged his shoulders. "I'm not afraid to work here. I faced the Nazis. I fought in hand-to-hand combat during the war. I promise you, I can do this job," Dovid said.

"Okey dokey! You're hired then. Cool Breeze will help you learn everything. He's my right-hand man. Smart as a whip that man is."

Dovid started work the next day. As he got to know his frequent customers, he found that he liked many of them. They were a lot kinder than the Nazis or the Communists. He didn't see rays of hatred coming from their eyes. For the most part, they were accepting of him, even with his white skin and Russian accent. It was true—as Arnie had promised—there were fights and occasional deaths at the bar; sometimes the fights were due to drugs or money, but many times they were also because of love triangles.

The hours were long. Dovid started at four in the afternoon

and closed the bar at four in the morning. By the time he finished cleaning up it was five. He arrived home just as the sun was rising.

One afternoon before the evening rush began, Dovid and Cool Breeze were drinking colas outside on the stoop in the backyard behind the building.

"You know it's not so different being a Jew than it is being colored," Dovid said. "People hate Jews for no reason other than that we are Jewish. They hate us even without ever meeting us, the same way that some white people hate or fear colored people."

"Yeah, lots of white folks has lots of fears. And they can be mean, that's for sure. I know you Jews don't have it easy, either. But the only difference between you and us is that you can hide your Jewishness. You see, Dovid, we can't hide what we is. It's right there on our faces. Folks know that we's colored as soon as they see our skin. Ain't no place to hide for us. We get paid less for doin' the same job as a white man. In the South we can't even drink from the same water fountain or ride in the front of a bus."

"Prejudice and hatred are terrible things, Cool Breeze. Their roots are based in fear. And, believe me, I know that it can kill. When I was a boy, I lived in Russia. That was when Hitler was in power. The Nazis came into Kiev where I grew up and shot the Jewish people, murdering them by the thousands. They buried their bodies in a large unmarked hole in the ground. They treated human beings like they were garbage.

"I was only thirteen when I enlisted in the Russian army and fought to defeat the Nazis. When the war ended, I was there with a platoon of men when we liberated the concentration camps. It was a horrific sight. Those camps were built to murder and to destroy human life. When I was there I saw piles of bodies; thousands of murdered men, women, and children. Their only crime was being Jewish."

"They only killed Jews?"

"Oh no, not just Jews. They killed as many Jews as they could get their hands on, but they killed plenty of other people too. They killed millions. Jehovah's Witnesses, homosexuals, Romany, Catholics, and so many more. They murdered the handicapped and the insane. For no reason at all, no reason. Such a terrible waste of life," Dovid said.

"When I was a kid, my folks and I was traveling through Texas. I saw a man with black skin like mine. He was dangling from a tree by a rope twisted around his neck. His eyes was bulging out and I could see that he wet his pants. From where I stood, I knowd that he was dead. There was a large wooden cross with burnt edges sticking in the ground right next to him. I asked my parents what had happened there. Why was that man dead with the cross of Jesus right by him and all? You see, my mama was a real church-going Christian and she wore a cross around her neck every day. I couldn't understand why whoever killed that man put a cross by him when a cross stood for Jesus and Jesus taught kindness and to love thy neighbor and such. My mama told me that certain people does things like twist and turn the Bible so that they can make it say what they wants it to say. That way they can kill folks who they don't like and do it in the name of good. Hitler wanted to kill Jews. He found a way to twist things until he made it look like he was doin' right. Or at least he did among his own folks, them other Nazis. I learned that the men who hung that poor fella was KKK. You know what that is? That be Klu Klux Klan. They be true evil.

13

They wanted to kill coloreds, so they twisted and turned things until they found a way to make it okay to kill anybody with dark skin. No matter what they say, it still don't make it right though."

"No, it doesn't. It's never right to hurt or mistreat another human being," Dovid said.

Working at the bar, David found that he loved jazz and blues. Many of the singers and musicians who came in to have a drink and sing a song or two were famous. At night, when one of the trumpet players picked up his horn and began to play a solo, Dovid felt as if the musician had opened a door into the depths of his own talented soul and taken the entire audience inside.

After a few weeks, Dovid began to invite Cool Breeze to come for dinner at his apartment on Sunday, when the bar was closed.

Since they'd come to the United States, Dovid and Eidel lived in a modest apartment on the fourth floor of a five-story walk-up on the South Side of Chicago. Dovid had plans for the future. He wanted children and he wanted them to have a house with a yard where they could run and play. And so Dovid had been squirreling away every extra penny to fulfill his dream. He was going to buy a house in the suburbs. It would be a long commute to work and he didn't have a car, but it was less expensive to buy north of the city than to buy a home in Chicago. He'd heard people talk about a suburb called Skokie. It was approximately forty-five minutes north of downtown. He read newspaper articles that said a lot of Jewish immigrants from Europe and Russia were moving there. Dovid thought that it would be a good place to start a family.

14

CHAPTER TWO

Eidel

Eidel thought about her mother every day. Her memories of Helen still overwhelmed her. Even though she was married, she not only missed her mother but she yearned for the life she had known before she left Poland. She didn't think she would, but she did. She missed the building where she grew up, and all of her neighbors. She missed her friends and she missed the church she attended with her mother every Sunday. Dovid was a kind, gentle, and loving husband but he was not around very much. She understood that he was busy working, trying to support them. He told her constantly that his plan was to give them a better life than they'd ever known. But Eidel felt as if she were living alone in a strange and intimidating place. Their neighbors were mostly Jewish immigrants who spoke Yiddish. People in the neighborhood, mostly the women, stood outside their apartments chatting in Yiddish during the afternoon. Eidel smiled at them when she went to the butcher or the bakery shop, but she never stopped to introduce herself. She was too self-conscious; besides, she couldn't speak a word of Yiddish. She was having a hard enough time trying to communicate in English. It seemed to Eidel that the other women were a close-knit group and she was an outsider. She'd talked to Dovid about having a child. A child, she thought, would fill her time and her heart, but Dovid insisted that they wait until he had enough money to buy the house and was sure that he could provide their children with a good life.

Dovid wanted to join the local synagogue. Eidel thought it was a waste of money. "We are trying so hard to save for this house that you want. Why would we join a synagogue?"

"Because we can! We can make friends and live the life my parents would have wanted for me," he said. "Here in America we can be openly Jewish." It made him so happy that she agreed to join as soon as they had extra money. He was hoping she would join the sisterhood and make friends but she was glad they were not members yet. She would never have felt comfortable going there without Dovid. She knew nothing about Judaism, nothing of the Jewish holidays or how to celebrate them. Even though Dovid and Eidel had spent a year in Israel before they were able to come to America, she still didn't understand or speak Hebrew or Yiddish. Typical Jewish food was foreign to her. And she found it difficult to relate to the other female members of the temple that lived in their neighborhood. The women were always nice to her. It wasn't that they were unwelcoming. But she felt so isolated, so lost. She missed celebrating Christmas and Easter. She wished she could go to mass with her mother. She longed to unburden herself in confession. She would have felt such relief telling a priest how guilty she felt for resenting Dovid for bringing her there to America only to abandon her by working such long hours. He was always gone, always leaving her alone. Intellectually, she knew that he couldn't help having to work. But emotionally, she felt lost. When he closed the door to leave for work at three each afternoon, her heart sank.

Eidel accepted that her birth mother was Jewish but she had been raised Catholic and she felt Catholic. How could she ever explain this to Dovid? He was so happy that he could be proud of his Jewish heritage in America. In fact, he had begun to wear a yarmulke all the time to show the world how proud he was of being a Jew. She was not ashamed of her background; she just couldn't find a way to fit in. Eidel had been raised as Ela and now Dovid expected her to forget everything she'd been brought up to know and love. She didn't know how to do that.

But she tried to be a good wife. She went to bed at eight every evening so she could set her alarm clock to wake her at 4 a.m. She did this so that she could have a light meal ready for David when he arrived at home. He usually came through the door at around six in the morning. She was so glad to see him that she felt she might explode with joy. Most mornings, they spent a little over an hour talking as he ate, then they made love. Afterwards, having worked all night, he fell into a deep sleep. All day he slept. Eidel tiptoed through the house, trying not to wake him. Then at two in the afternoon he got up, ate, showered, and dressed. He kissed her quickly and was off to work. Eidel was alone again.

Six days a week, every week, Dovid was gone to work from three in the afternoon until six in the morning. While Dovid slept in the morning, Eidel would go out to the market to buy food for the day. Otherwise, she was at home all day and evening where she felt like a prisoner in her apartment, alone and lost within her own mind.

When her mother died, she thought that she had wanted to get away from Warsaw and all the memories that hurt so deeply each time she saw them. But now that she was so far away from everything familiar, she longed to be back in Poland where she understood the language, where she had friends in the church, where she didn't feel so miserably

17

lonely and disconnected from everyone.

CHAPTER THREE

1961

Autumn brought a chilly breeze down from the north. Eidel liked the fresh brisk air on her face. It had been a long, sweaty, sleepy summer, and she was glad to finally get some relief from the relentless heat. Although she knew that fall was a prelude to the upcoming frigid chill and snow of a Chicago winter, she still loved the feeling of the change of season when the heat gave way to the cool winds that blew off of Lake Michigan in late September.

One morning, bored and alone, she walked to the bakery. She bought bread and a cake. It was good not to ever be hungry. Dovid was earning enough money for them to have plenty to eat. That was a blessing.

It is something to be thankful for.

As she continued walking, she passed a large Catholic church with beautifully colorful stained glass windows. She'd passed it before, but today she stopped to look up at the cross on the top.

Mama, I miss you so much, Eidel thought.

She had never been inside of a church in America. From the street, it looked like a medieval castle.

What would be the harm if I just went in for a little while? Dovid would never need to know.

She knew Dovid wouldn't be happy about her going into a church. He wanted her to embrace Judaism. And she was trying. She wanted to please him, but she longed to feel closer to the memory of her mother and she thought that being inside the church would bring her back to all that she'd once shared with Helen. So she climbed the stone stairs up to the front of the cathedral and opened the heavy door. When she walked inside, she was immediately transported to a time when she and her mother had gone to a church similar to that one. As rays of sunlight shot through the stained glass windows, rainbows appeared on the polished wood floor. Eidel sat down in a pew in the back row and looked up at the altar. Her eyes landed upon a large statue of Jesus on the cross. Burning tears fell on her cheeks.

I am so confused...and so alone.

She sat in the back at the end of the long wooden bench for a little over an hour. Her mind was traveling down memory lane the entire time. When she finally got up and left the church, she felt guilty for going inside but she also felt at peace. Being in the church had helped her to feel Helen's presence and she needed that. She desperately needed to feel her mother's hand in hers, even if her mother was only with her in spirit. For the first time since Eidel had come to America, she felt some relief from her loneliness.

But she didn't want to do anything to disappoint Dovid and so she vowed to herself that she would not go back. In fact, now that she'd gained some inner strength, she was determined to go to the synagogue and introduce herself. She would tell the rabbi that they were planning to join as soon as they could afford to. Yes, she would go; why not try to make friends? Two afternoons later, she walked to the Jewish temple that she and Dovid were thinking about joining. But once she got there she felt intimidated. Eidel lost her nerve and she didn't go inside. Instead, she went home. Dovid had been teaching her English and her language skills were improving. He had spent several hours on Sunday translating a book for her to study while he was at work during the week.

As she was walking home from the synagogue she felt defeated. But she told herself, *I'll go home and work on my English. Then I'll go back to the synagogue in a couple of months when I speak more fluent English. I will be able to communicate with everyone much better then. That will make it easier for me to make friends.*

Eidel walked quickly back to the safety of her apartment. She locked the door behind her and took a deep breath. She put up a pot of soup for Dovid to eat before he left for work and then she washed the floor for the third time that week.

CHAPTER FOUR

Arnie was right; the bar was not for the faint of heart. On a busy Saturday night, a loud argument began between two men, both of them very drunk. They cursed and pushed each other until they came to fisticuffs. One of the men swore the other had stolen his money. Fights were not an unusual occurrence; most of the time they ended with a couple of well-placed punches, a bruised ego, and a threat of future revenge. This time, things did not go as well. The man accused of stealing pulled a knife out of his pocket—a switchblade. He pressed a button and a long silver blade popped out of the base. It shimmered as it caught the light from the overhead bulb. Dovid was the first of the employees to see the knife and quickly jumped over the bar. He raced over to try to stop the fight.

Arnie yelled, "Get out of there, Dovi. You'll get hurt. Get back behind the bar. I'm calling the police."

But it was too late. Dovid's shoulder was already slashed. The cut was so deep that it didn't start to bleed right away. It took several minutes but then blood poured from the open wound. The two men were still fighting; Cool Breeze pulled Dovid out of the way. By the time the police arrived, one of the men was dead, and Dovid had to go to the hospital where he received twelve stitches.

CHAPTER FIVE

It was easy to see that Eidel was becoming depressed. Dovid knew it was because she was alone so much. He gave a lot of thought to how he might help her adjust to living in America. She couldn't get a job because all she knew how to do was secretarial work and her English wasn't good enough for her to do that. She couldn't even sell at a department store because of her language skills. He'd asked her if she wanted to take classes to help her learn faster, but she refused. It was then that he'd insisted that they join the synagogue. They would have to dip into their savings to pay for the membership, but he was hopeful that it would help her meet other women. However, when he suggested she join the sisterhood, she just shook her head. Dovid tried to attend Saturday services with Eidel when he could, but the tavern was busy on Friday and Saturday nights and, quite frankly, he was too tired in the morning to go anywhere. It was all he could do to take a hot shower and collapse into his bed. If he had been religious, he would never have worked on Friday night and Saturday. However, Dovid had lived most of his life without religion and although he loved being a Jew, he was more of a Jew by nationality than by religion. He needed his job and so he worked whenever his boss needed him. When he and Eidel came to America, Dovid vowed to himself that he was going to provide well for his family. He would not be satisfied with an apartment in a lower-middle-class neighborhood. He was willing to work hard, as hard as was necessary, in order to build a good life for his wife and future children. Dovid might have been busy and distracted by the demands of his job, but he loved his wife and, more than anything, he wanted her to be happy. He could see how sad she was and Eidel's depression weighed heavily upon him. Dovid needed to do something to help her, but what? Then God sent a solution in the most unlikely of ways.

Cool Breeze didn't show up for work on one Thursday night. He did not come to work on Friday or Saturday, either. Dovid was worried but he had no idea how to reach him. Then, on Saturday at about 6 p.m., just a few hours before the evening rush was to begin, Arnie called Dovid into the back room.

"Listen, take my car over to the flophouses on Madison and Morgan. You know where that is?"

"I think so. About a mile west of downtown?"

"Yeah. Go to the third building from the corner on the south side of Madison. There is a little restaurant there; it's a greasy spoon-type of grill. You can't miss it. Outside, right above the joint, is a big sign in black letters that says 'Mike's Home Cooked Food.' You'll see it. Upstairs of the restaurant is a hotel; a flophouse, really. Go on into the restaurant. There's a nice fella in there who works for Mike Marshall who owns most of the buildings, the restaurant too. Anyway, the fella who runs the restaurant for Mike is Harry Rosen. Tell Harry I sent you to find Breeze. He'll understand, and he'll know where Breeze is. Don't worry, Harry will take you right up to Cool Breeze's room."

"Cool Breeze lives in a flophouse?"

"Yeah. I pay him pretty good for a colored man, and he's a great fella, real smart, and real capable, but the problem is that he drinks and shoots all his money up his arm. He's got a bad heroin habit, Dovi. You're probably gonna find him in a pretty bad state. Here's what you do, are you listening?"

"Yes."

"Breeze is probably gonna be passed out. So, you gotta pick him up and take him to the bathroom down the hall. When you get there, turn on the cold water in the shower and put him in there. Make sure Breeze's head is under the cold water and stays there until he comes to. Once he's conscious, put him the car and bring him here."

Dovid nodded and took the keys to Arnie's car. He didn't even have an Illinois driver's license but he got into Glassman's new Cadillac and drove thirty-one blocks to the part of town that was known as skid row. Arnie was right; it was easy to find the restaurant. Dovid walked inside. There was a circular counter with a man close to his age standing behind it, wiping his hands with a dishrag. Two disheveled men were eating French fries at the far end of the counter.

"Take a seat anywhere," the man with the dishrag said.

Dovid sat several seats away from the other two customers.

From where he sat, Dovid could see the dirty grill. A tall, thick man with light brown skin and long, straight black hair in a ponytail was flipping a burger. At the man's waist, Dovid noticed, was a belt with a pouch that held a Bowie knife.

"You must be Harry Rosen? Arnie Glassman sent me," Dovid said.

"I *am* Harry Rosen. By the way, allow me to introduce the best cook on Madison. This is Joey Onefeather," Harry said, indicating toward the cook with the knife.

"Nice to meet you both," Dovid said.

"Are you a new bus driver?" Rosen asked.

"No. I don't know what you're talking about," Dovid answered.

"Oh, right next door is the Grayline headquarters. You know what that is?"

"Can't say I do." Dovid shook his head.

"It's a special bus line. All it does is pick up the rich folks after they had their dinner at the ritzy Blackhawk restaurant and then scoot them right through our lovely part of town and drop them off safely at the stadium so they can go and see the Blackhawks play. Rich folks love hockey. Can't say I don't enjoy it, too. Once in a while, the drivers get an extra ticket to the game and they give it to me. But, God forbid, the sheltered rich people from Michigan Avenue should have to come through our part of the city all alone. Hell, they sure don't want to know how the other half lives.

"And," he gestured to the area outside the window where a prostitute in a tight red dress was arguing price with a potential customer. "Who can blame them? Anyway, sometimes the bus drivers come into our lovely little establishment to grab a bite. When I saw you, I just thought you might be a new driver. I guess not."

Harry shrugged.

"So what will you have?" he asked. "Menu is up there on the blackboard. Food's not fancy, but it's good."

"Thanks, but I am not here to eat. I am looking for Crawford B. Dell. Arnie Glassman sent me to see you. He said you would know where to find Mr. Dell."

"Any friend of Arnie's is a friend of mine. Great fella, that Arnie. Crawford B. Dell is here. He is staying in room 402. I am assuming, since you mentioned Arnie and he works for Arnie, you work with both of them at the tavern?"

"Yeah."

"Well, I should let you know that Dell owes money for rent. Plenty of money. He hasn't paid in a while and Mike, my boss, is planning to throw him out."

"How much does he owe?" Dovid asked.

"Forty dollars for all of last month and half of this month."

Dovid pulled out his wallet.

I am not made of money. I have to try and save for my own family, he thought angrily. But he wasn't going to let them kick Cool Breeze out on the street. He would have asked Cool Breeze to come and stay with him, but Dovid's apartment was so small there was hardly enough room for him and Eidel.

"You're gonna pay his rent?"

"Yeah. That's what it looks like," Dovid said handing the money to Harry.

"That's really nice of you. I'm sorry I don't even know your name," Harry said.

"Dovid Levi"

"Cool Breeze is a good person and he's a smart man. He just has a real bad addiction problem."

"Drugs and alcohol right? I know. Arnie told me."

"Yeah, it's a real shame. He's a typical addict. You'd be surprised how many smart people live here in the flop who are in the same situation. They lose everything, their homes their families, everything."

"I can imagine," Dovid said.

"It's easy to get mixed up with that stuff when you can't see any future, you're stuck in a dead-end job, and nobody is willing to help you."

"I'm a Jew, and it's not easy for us to find work and to find our way. I got lucky, Arnie is Jewish too. But it was hard to find a good job," Dovid said. "And as difficult as it was for me, I feel that it's even harder for a colored man. No matter how smart he is, how hard he tries, it seems like the world keeps him down. Even good people seem to feel it's all right to keep the colored man down. I don't understand it."

Dovid added, "Do you know what I mean?"

Dovid was remembering how Arnie Glassman had said, "I pay him good for a colored man."

Why should a colored man be treated differently than a white man? This behavior is no different than Jews being treated like they were worth less than non-Jews. But Arnie is a Jew, how is it possible that Arnie can't see this parallel?

"Yes, I actually do agree with you. I think the way the colored people are treated has pushed many of them to think that they are stuck, that no matter what they do, they will never be treated like equals."

"I could be wrong, but I think I hear a Polish accent. Are you from Poland?" Dovid asked.

"Yes, both my wife and I are from Poland. How did you know it was a Polish accent?"

"My wife is Polish," Dovid smiled.

Dovid caught a glimpse of the dark numbers tattooed on Harry's arm. "You were in a concentration camp?"

Harry looked away. "I met my wife Ida in Auschwitz."

Dovid nodded.

"Were you in a camp?"

"No. I fought for the Russian army. But I am a Jew. And I am proud to be a Jew. Harry, I was just a boy when I saw my parents executed by the Nazis. So even though I wasn't imprisoned in a camp, I too have suffered."

For a few moments there was an uncomfortable silence. Then Dovid said, "So, Harry. it was a pleasure to meet you. I am going up to room 402 now."

"Wait ..." Harry said. Dovid turned around. "I know this is a strange thing to ask, but we are both immigrants and, well, maybe you and your wife would like to come for dinner at my apartment. You see, I work long hours and my wife gets lonely. I thought perhaps since your wife is from Poland and she speaks Polish maybe our wives could be friends."

Here it is, my solution to Eidel's loneliness. God sent a miracle, Dovid thought. *This is exactly what Eidel needs; a lady friend who speaks her native language.*

"We would love to come. I work six days, but I am off on Sunday."

"I am usually off on Monday and Tuesday, but we close early on Sunday, so Sunday night will be perfect. Here is my address. Is six o'clock good for you?"

"Six is perfect because I am off all day."

"By the way, I have to tell you that Ida and I don't keep

kosher. I don't know if you and your wife do…"

"No, we don't either."

"This will be nice for all of us. I think our wives will get along very well. I'm looking forward to Sunday."

"So am I," Dovid said as he walked out of the restaurant. He entered the vestibule where the stairs to the hotel rooms were located and began to climb up the stairs to room number 402. As he did, Dovid looked up as if he were looking to the heavens and not at the top floor of a flophouse. He smiled and winked at God as he whispered, "Thank you."

CHAPTER SIX

Dovid knocked on the door to room 402 but there was no answer. He waited and tried again, then went back downstairs to the office.

"Harry, do you have a master key? Crawford isn't answering the door," Dovid asked.

"Yes, I have one. Let me take you up." Harry followed Dovid back to Cool Breeze's room.

When the door opened, the smell of sweat and mold turned Dovid's stomach. It was only a week before Halloween and winter had not yet sent her icy winds flying off the lake and through the city. If it had been colder, the stench might not have been as strong. But the temperature outside was a pleasant sixty degrees. Dovid rushed over and opened the window quickly to let in some fresh air.

It was a single room, dark and damp. The floor was made of gray concrete. He saw Cool Breeze lying on a dirty mattress covered in dark stains and bare of sheets or blankets.

The stains are probably shit or blood, Dovid thought, willing himself not to gag. *I've been in the army where I've seen death and worked with my father in medicine and yet a scene like this one can still make me want to vomit.*

Cool Breeze was naked to the waist. He wore only a pair of soiled boxer shorts. His head hung over the side of the bed. On the floor were several empty wine bottles. A rubber band was tied around the top of his arm. A little lower down, an empty syringe hung like a marionette by a needle still in his vein. A small pool of blood had turned dark on the floor.

Dovid checked for a pulse. Cool Breeze was still alive.

Carefully, Dovid removed the needle, holding the point of insertion to prevent additional bleeding. He had nothing to cover the wound. Dovid couldn't stay there holding a wound. He had to do something to wake his friend out of his comatose state or he was afraid Cool Breeze might die. Although Cool Breeze was thin, it was difficult to lift a full-grown man who was limp dead weight. But with Harry's help, together they carried Cool Breeze down the hall to the bathroom. Once there, Dovid turned on the shower. The water was very cold. He and Harry put Cool Breeze under the running water. At first, Cool Breeze didn't move, he just laid there. Then a minute later, Breeze jumped to life. He started shaking, his body jiving in protest against being startled by the freezing water.

"Hey, you tryin' to kill me?" Cool Breeze said.

"I'm trying to help you," Dovid said.

"Mr. Dovi, how did you find me?" Cool Breeze's eyes were glassy, but he recognized his friend.

"Arnie sent me."

"That Arnie."

Cool Breeze laughed, even though he was shaking violently from the shock of the cold water. "Get me the hell out of here." He got up but was unsteady and slipped back down in the shower stall.

Dovid and Harry helped Cool Breeze to his feet.

"Let's put on your clothes and then we'll go to the tavern," Dovid said. "You have other underwear?"

"Ain't got none," Cool Breeze said.

"You'll have to do without," Dovid said.

"I have a clean shirt downstairs in the back of the restaurant in case I spill something on my shirt. No pants though. And no underwear," Harry said. "But I can give the shirt to you for Dell. At least it's clean."

"I owe you, my friend," Dovid said.

"Think nothing of it."

Harry left and went downstairs. He came back a few minutes later with a towel and a shirt with worn cuffs. "Here, dry yourself off and get dressed," Harry said to Cool Breeze.

"Listen, Harry. I promise you I am gonna get you your rent as soon as I go in to work," Cool Breeze said.

"He paid it, Dell," Harry said, pointing to Dovid. "Give the money back to him."

"I will. You'll see, Dovi. I will. I promise you, I am gonna do just that."

Dovid knew he would never see his money again, but his heart was breaking to see a man as brilliant as Cool Breeze wasting away. He wished he could help him, but he knew that there was nothing he could do except be a friend. Cool Breeze dried himself off. The shirt Harry gave him was newer and cleaner than his other one, and so he wore it. Once Cool Breeze was dressed, he and Dovid walked towards the car. On the ground was a big puddle of dark red blood.

"That sure looks like blood," Dovi said.

"Probably is," Cool Breeze said. "Lots of times folks gets killed around here and don't nobody care. The police don't even come so ain't no use to call 'em."

Dovid understood what it was like to live under a corrupt government. He just hadn't expected to find a police department like that in America, the greatest country in the world.

Dovid and Cool Breeze got into Arnie's Cadillac and began driving toward the tavern.

"I hope you realize that you could have died from what you did. You could have overdosed and died," Dovid said.

"Yeah, I knows it. I'm gonna quit. You see, Mr. Dovi, I been planning on it. I'm gonna be quitten' right after the first of the year."

Dovid shook his head. He knew that Cool Breeze wished he could quit but he wasn't able. "How did you ever get involved with heroin?"

"My pusher give me my first fix for free. Now he charges me a fucking fortune. I was a stupid kid that first time. The bastard promised me that I couldn't get hooked by trying it just once. Boy, was he wrong. I was afraid of needles back in them days so he done for me that first time. I gotta tell you that it was like being in heaven. I ain't never felt nothin' like it. It made me feel good all over. But don't you ever try it, Dovi. You know why? Because you is gonna get hooked right away, I can sure promise you that. And, you know what else? No matter what you do, you can never hit that first-time high again. You see, after you had that high, somethin' like a devil inside you make you just keep on tryin' to feel that same way again, but no matter how much smack you shoot, you can't

34

get there never again."

"Well, don't worry about me trying it. I have no intentions of doing that. Will you tell me who your pusher is?"

"I ain't gonna tell you. Cause ifin' I tell you, you gonna kill him or have him arrested. I know you, Dovi."

"You're right I am. It would be my pleasure," Dovid said. He was seething with anger.

They rode in silence for a few minutes. Then Dovid said, "Cool Breeze, was it a white man?"

"Was what a white man?"

"The pusher? The man who got you started on heroin."

"What difference do it make?"

"It makes a difference to me. I want to know."

"Yeah, he white."

Dovid shook his head. "What can I do to convince you to tell me who he is?"

"Ain't nothin' you can do. I ain't never gonna tell you."

"Damn it," Dovid said under his breath.

CHAPTER SEVEN

Sunday at 5:30 p.m., Dovid and Eidel walked four blocks west until they got to the Rosen's apartment. On the way, they stopped at *Miriam Goldberg's Bread and Sweets* and picked up a cake. At first, Eidel didn't want to go. She was shy and uncomfortable going to the home of strangers. But Dovid convinced her that she would enjoy herself. She was nervous, afraid the Rosens wouldn't like her. Dovid had told her that the Rosens were Jewish and that they were from Poland. He explained that Harry and Ida had been in a concentration camp. She wondered if either of them knew Zofia Weiss. She also worried that they would be able to tell that she had not been raised as a Jew and that they would reject her.

When the Levis arrived, Ida spoke to Eidel in Polish. It was so easy for Eidel to converse in her own native language. Because of this, Eidel began to feel comfortable. Eidel offered to help with the meal preparation and by the time the food was on the table, the two women were fast friends.

There was never a lull in the conversation. The women shared recipes; the men discussed the handsome American President Kennedy. Both couples agreed that they wanted to move out of the city as soon as they could afford it and live in the suburbs. Dovid and Eidel talked about having children, and that drove the conversation to a darker place. Ida opened up and told the Levis that she had been experimented on while in Auschwitz and because of a doctor named Mengele, who was a sadist, she could not have children. When Ida and

Harry talked about the Nazis and the concentration camps Eidel didn't feel uncomfortable. She wasn't ready to tell them about her past but it was all too confusing, too painful. She folded and unfolded her napkin as she listened to their sad stories.

"We knew each other from the neighborhood when we were children," Harry said, referring to himself and Ida. "Both of our families had been sent to the Lodz Ghetto. I didn't see Ida again until I was transferred to Auschwitz. By then, my entire family was dead. Later, I learned that Ida had also been transferred with her sister. I only saw her across a fence for a few seconds. We were not able to speak to each other. But she smiled at me, and you see, I hadn't seen a friendly face from the old neighborhood in so long that when I saw her it made me feel like there might be something waiting for me at the end of all this. That is, if I could survive."

"I can still remember that day when I saw Harry," Ida said. "He smiled back at me. I wanted to hear his voice and remember what life was like when we were still free to laugh and play and sing. But there was no laughter for me because my sister and I were a part of Mengele's chosen children. We were his human experiments. He tortured us daily. But while she was alive there was still a chance that we might survive and go on together. Of course, that was not to be."

Harry patted Ida's hand. "Every day I would think about Ida and daydream about what our lives would be like once we were free. It helped me to get through some of the most terrible things a human being can endure. By the time we were liberated, I knew I loved her and I knew I wanted to marry her," Harry said.

"The day the camp was liberated, I was sitting outside in a corner with my back against a building. I was just a child. All alone now, my sister was dead. I was thirteen at the time; Harry was seventeen. Most of the children in the camp didn't survive. But, because my sister Ana and I were twins, Mengele selected us. I had a wonderful sister; she was my best friend. I guess I should explain this better. Mengele was the camp doctor; he should rot in hell. He liked to use twins for his experiments, especially children. And this doctor... he was the most sadistic bastard that ever lived. Somehow I survived his prodding, poking, surgeries without anesthetic. But my sister, my Ana, she was a delicate little soul. She should rest in peace ... she didn't make it. "

"So," Harry said. "It was a bright sunny day when the soldiers came marching in. To us, they looked like gods in their uniforms. You're free," they told us. "You're free. I remember I was crying. All around me prisoners were on their knees, kissing the soldiers' feet," Harry said, his face contorted with the recollection.

Dovid remembered the liberations, too, because he had been one of the soldiers that freed several camps. It was strange for Dovid to hear these events brought to life by two of the prisoners so many years later. Dovid could have told Harry that he was one of the soldiers, not at Auschwitz, but at three other camps. However, he decided not to say anything.

"It was over. It was finally over! I touched my arm; I touched my leg. You see, I couldn't believe that I was alive. I felt almost like I shouldn't be. Then, in many ways, I felt guilty that I was. Everyone I loved was dead. So many others had perished, too. I was walking around in a daze. I was not sure what I was going to do next. But then I saw Ida sitting in the corner with her back up against that dirty gray building.

38

She was so small and looked so all alone and lost that the sight of her made my heart ache. I remembered how lively she had been when we were little children in the old neighborhood. It was very strange, but a vision of a day very long ago came to me. I remembered when all the children who lived on our street were skating at the park. Ida was good on skates. This was a strange thing to recall on the day of our liberation. However, as I looked at her I could see the little girl she'd been before the Nazis destroyed us, laughing as she whirled across the ice. You see, although I'd kept her in my mind all this time, I didn't know her story. We had never spoken. At the time, I just assumed that she'd lost her whole family in the camp. I knew I had lost mine. So I went over to her and sat down beside her. I didn't know what I was going to say. I only knew that I had to talk to her."

"I was so glad he came over to me. It was so good to see a familiar face. I started to cry, to weep, really. He held me in his arms," Ida said.

"We got married a year later. Then, for two years after that, we lived at a displaced persons camp. It was really a liberated concentration camp that the Red Cross had set up for us because we had no place else to go. The Jewish Committee helped Ida and me come to America. My father's sister and her husband lived here in Chicago and they sponsored us. We lived with them for about eight months. Ida and I found odd jobs here and there until Mike hired me. It was lucky for me that my father was a professor at the University in Poland and had taught me English. It helped me a lot to be able to speak the language in America. I have been teaching Ida to speak better English but she still likes to speak in Polish." Harry smiled at his wife and took her hand across the table.

"I am used to speaking Polish. I am comfortable with it. But

39

I am happy to learn the language of this great country that has given us a home," Ida said, smiling.

After listening to the Rosens speak, Eidel understood much better why Zofia had sent her away from the Warsaw Ghetto.

By the time Eidel and Dovid were on their way home, Eidel was talking about inviting the Rosens to their house the following Sunday.

The couples became friends. But more importantly, as Dovid had hoped, Eidel and Ida spent much of their free time together. They tried new recipes, made tablecloths, sewed, knitted, but most of all they found a friendship that bound them like sisters to each other.

CHAPTER EIGHT

December 1961

Cool Breeze seemed to be doing much better. He hadn't missed work again since the incident when Dovid had found him passed out in his room. For this, Dovid was glad. He tried to make himself believe that perhaps he'd been wrong and Cool Breeze had actually found the strength to quit shooting heroin.

Business had slowed down.

"Don't worry fellas, it's always slower in the winter," Arnie told them. But when Dovid looked at Arnie Glassman, he could see that Arnie wasn't feeling well. Dovid didn't know if it was because of the lack of customers or if Arnie was ill. Dovid and Cool Breeze both tried to do whatever they could in order to make Arnie feel better. Instead of sitting around, they tried to look busy. They cleaned the refrigerators. Not that the refrigerators were dirty, but they wanted to appear busy so that Arnie wouldn't see them doing nothing.

When Hanukkah came, Dovid bought a gold hair clip for Eidel, which he wrapped carefully in a few pages of the Sun-Times newspaper. They'd purchased a menorah when they were in Israel; it was the closest thing they could find to the one that Dovid's parents had when he was a child. Dovid was excited about giving his wife her gift. Hanukkah was not for another week, but he had the gift in his pocket when he returned from work. He longed to give it to her, to see the smile on her face. It was a beautiful 14k gold hair clip with several small pearls and amethyst running along the side. She would love it. He knew how much she enjoyed wearing pretty hair ornaments, but she'd never owned one that was real gold. He could hardly wait to give it to her.

As always, she had his food ready when he got home from work that morning. He took his shower and then sat down at the table.

"How was your night?" she asked.

"It was good. Slow, but good. It's cold outside. People don't want to go out of their homes, I guess."

"Ida was here yesterday afternoon and we made these perogies. Do you like them?"

"Yes, they're very good. You like Ida."

"I do. I am glad that the Rosens are our friends."

"So am I."

"I have some good news. I talked to Harry today. He got four free tickets to a Blackhawks game from one of the bus drivers who comes into the restaurant all the time. He wants to know if we want to go with him and Ida. What do you say?" Dovid asked. Harry had called him that afternoon and told him about the tickets.

"I don't know what a Blackhawks game is. But I will have a good time because Ida will be there."

Dovid let out a laugh. "I should have told you. The Blackhawks are Chicago's hockey team. Have you ever seen a hockey game?"

"No…" She smiled.

"It will be a lot of fun. I'll explain what's going on as we watch the game. You'll like it."

"When are the ticket's for?"

"The first week in January, on a Sunday afternoon. Harry said that he switched days with Mike's nephew, Ralph, so that he could go. I don't think I had a chance to tell you about Ralph."

"You never mentioned him," she said.

"Well, Harry was upset because he lost some hours when Mike had to hire Ralph, who is Mike's sister's kid. Mike said he had no choice. It's family; he had to give Ralph a job. What a bum this Ralph is. From what I hear, he's been fired from every job he has had. The kid's gotten into trouble with the law for gambling a few times, too. Harry says he heard that Ralph was also arrested for stealing. The kid's a real no good. And the worst of it is that because the kid couldn't get another job, Mike had to take some days away from Harry to make room for his nephew. And of course, that means a cut in pay for Harry."

"Ida never told me," Eidel said.

"She probably didn't want to upset you.

"If we have to help the Rosens out financially, I would agree to it," Eidel said.

"We'll see. I already asked Harry how he was going to get along. He said that they have some money saved. He says they'll get by. They don't seem to want our help."

"You asked him?"

"In a round-about way, yes, I asked him. And we'll help them if it comes to that. But that's probably why Ida never mentioned it to you. She didn't want you to feel obligated to offer them a loan."

"Oh, I feel so bad for them," Eidel said.

"Well, there is a bright side," Dovid said.

"Oh? And what is that?"

"At least Harry can get off work all day on a Sunday. So we can all go to the hockey game. It will be a lot of fun."

Dovid looked up from his plate and smiled at her. Then he winked. "We'll make a day of it. The game starts at one. We'll leave early and take the bus over to Taylor Street. I know this little Italian restaurant that has the most delicious Italian beef sandwiches. After lunch we can all hop on a bus back to the stadium."

She smiled at him. "I think you're right, Dovid, it's going to be a great day. I think I'll love the Italian beef and the hockey."

"I know you will," he said and began eating his meal.

For a few minutes she watched him. How handsome he was in her eyes, even though he was more than ten years her senior. She was proud that he was her husband. Dovid had adjusted so well to life in America. And now, because of his friends, she was feeling better about being there in the U.S.

Eidel had something she had to tell him and she was afraid he would be angry or disappointed in her. However, there was no getting around it, she had to tell him. She steeled herself before she spoke.

"Dovid?" she said, her voice a little above a whisper.

"Yes, love?" he said, putting down his fork and looking into her eyes.

She looked away.

"I have something to tell you. I hope you won't be mad."

Dovid wiped his lips with the napkin. "Mad? Why? What is it Eidel?"

"Oh Dovid…"

She was wringing a dishtowel in her hands. He looked at her with genuine concern. Then she continued speaking. "I don't know how it happened. We were so careful. I know you said you wanted to wait until we had a house. I am sorry; it's probably all my fault. I am sure that there must have been something I should have done to prevent it better. I didn't have any prior experience, so I didn't know what to do. Please, Dovid, don't be mad…."

"Eidel? Are you trying to tell me what I think you are trying to tell me?"

"I'm pregnant. I am sorry, Dovi."

"Don't be sorry," he said and got up from the table, his napkin falling to the floor. Dovid lifted her in his arms.

"It's maybe a little bit sooner than we originally wanted but what a mitzvah. Thanks be to God! I will go to the shul and give a donation tomorrow in thanks for this great blessing. Oh, my darling, how can I be mad? After all, we have been touched by God. You and I are going to have a child." He kissed her all over her face. She was crying tears of joy.

"I'm so glad you're happy about it. I want a child, Dovid. I want one more than I can ever tell you. I was just afraid that you would be upset because it happened before we had a

45

house. But when I look at poor Ida and I know she can never have children my heart breaks. The bond between a mother and child is the deepest bond any woman can ever have. Thank you for being happy about this."

"The bond between a father and his children is also a great gift. Thank you for being the mother of my future children. I love you, Eidel." He whispered into her ear, "Oh, and by the way, since you gave me my Hanukkah gift early, which of course is this wonderful blessing of a precious little life growing inside of you…" He leaned over and gently caressed her belly.

"Let me give you your gift early, too."

Dovid took the box with the hair clip out of the breast pocket of his shirt and laid it on the table.

"Open it," he said.

Eidel opened the box and looked at the beautiful piece of jewelry. Tears filled her eyes.

"Do you like it?" Dovid asked.

"I love it," Eidel said, holding the box to her chest. "Dovid … do you like my gift?"

"A child, a blessing, nu? What's not to love? Of course, I am very happy. God bless you, my sweet darling. I am going to be a father!" Then he carried her into the bedroom and made tender love to her.

CHAPTER NINE

The winter was cold and unforgiving. Scraping the ice off of the car in the morning and shoveling the walk when he couldn't find anyone to pay to do it was taking its toll on Arnie Glassman. By the time Arnie arrived at work he was red-faced, out of breath, and exhausted. He began to come in late because he would wait until he could find a boy on his way to school and offer to pay him to shovel the snow. When he tried to do it himself, he got chest pain and was unable to breathe.

Arnie had no children and his wife had passed away several years ago. His work was all that was left. Arnie's father had come from Romania, a poor immigrant who raised himself to the status of a five-star vendor in the South Water market, selling fruit and vegetables. Unlike most of Arnie's peers, Arnie's family had plenty of money. Because his mother had died in childbirth and his father had never been able to bring himself to remarry, Arnie was an only child.

His father adored his son and wanted a better life for him than getting up early every morning and working at the market. He wanted Arnie to have an education. After all, that was why William Glassman, better known as Willie, had come to America. He yearned to escape the poverty of Europe. He longed for his son to be an educated and important man. This was an opportunity Willie would have relished had it ever been presented to him. However, the only option Willie had was to steal away from Europe on a voyage to the U.S. and when he got the chance to do so, Willie didn't hesitate.

He met Arnie's mother on the ship and fell instantly in love with the beautiful, spirited young girl. She was very young and traveling with her sister. Their parents had spent every penny they had to send their two daughters to America, where the streets were lined with gold. Bessie and her sister, Fannie were both beautiful girls but in Willie's mind, Bessie was the prettier one. He was smitten as soon as he saw her.

Willie was bold. He knew that all he had was three dollars in his pocket, but he vowed to her that if she married him he would give her a good life and someday she would be a wealthy woman. He too, was very young but still older than her by five years. Bessie liked his confidence. He was confident almost to the point of arrogance and it amused her. She also liked his handsome strong jawline and deep-set eyes.

Willie and Bessie were married as soon as they both passed through Ellis Island. Fannie had nowhere to go, so Bessie insisted that her sister live with her and Willie. Willie didn't mind. He was happy to indulge his beautiful wife. He worked long hours in a physically demanding job, but he was young and he was tireless; perhaps that was where Arnie inherited his own work ethic. With the help a few good business breaks, Willie made good on his promise.

Bessie was a wealthy woman by the time she got pregnant with Arnie. Willie hired women in the neighborhood to help his wife during her pregnancy. This was a luxury few women of their class could afford. However, women died in childbirth all the time and Willie was worried because Bessie was a tiny, delicate girl. He wanted to make sure she had whatever she needed to make the pregnancy easier on her.

Then Fannie met a man, got married, and moved to New York. It devastated Bessie to have her sister so far away during her pregnancy. Willie promised that as soon as the baby was born they would travel to visit her sister. This seemed to pacify Bessie. When Arnie was born with the help of the local midwife, Willie was overcome with joy. His first child...a son! They named the boy for Willie's grandfather, Arnold Glassman. At first, Bessie was thriving. In fact, her skin was glowing and she was excited to take her son to New York to visit her sister. The woman whom Willie had hired was helping Bessie pack when Bessie suddenly felt feverish and tired. She told the housekeeper that she had to lie down. By the time Arnie's father got home, she was dead.

"Childbed fever," the housekeeper told Willie. Willie was distraught. He couldn't believe that just that morning, Bessie had been fine and now she was gone from his life forever. He wanted to resent the child who had taken his beloved wife, but he couldn't. When Willie looked into his son's tiny face and counted the little boy's fingers and toes, a wave of love came over him. He would raise this boy and give him a great life filled with opportunities that he never had.

When Arnie was old enough his father insisted that he get a college education. It didn't matter to Willie that Arnie had no desire to go on in school. He had the grades and he got accepted, and Willie refused to take no for an answer. His son would be educated!

Arnie was smart. He was accepted into the University of Chicago where he joined a fraternity. It was easy for Arnie to drink all night and still keep up his grades. It was on just such a morning that Arnie received a phone call. One of his frat brothers came to his room and knocked on the door. Arnie's head ached from a hangover.

"You have a phone call, Glassman," his frat brother said.

"Yeah, all right. I'll be right there." Arnie sat up in bed; his head was pounding. "I gotta stop drinking like this," he said aloud to himself and walked to the phone in the hall in his underwear.

"Yeah," Arnie said.

"Listen, it's Jake." Jake was Arnie's father's partner and best friend. "I got some bad news. Your father was bringing a truckload of grapefruit from Texas to Chicago. You know how God damn stubborn he is. I told him to stop but he drove through the night, and then went to see the vendor in the morning. He spent all day bargaining then loading the truck so he was dog-tired. He shoulda checked into a hotel, but I know your father, he didn't want to leave his load of goods on the back of the truck open and unattended. He was afraid his stuff would get stolen. Anyway, he headed back home to Chicago without getting any rest for two days. Sometime during the night, Willie musta fell asleep at the wheel and his truck veered into a tree, killing him instantly. I am sorry, Arnie. I really am."

Arnie was shaking. He couldn't believe his father was gone. The news was painful, very painful. However, in a way, it was also freeing. His father had been such a strong-willed man that Arnie had never dared to say no to him. Now Arnie could make his own decisions. He could quit attending the university. And since Willie had left his son with plenty of money, Arnie was now free to do whatever he wanted. All of his life, Arnie had loved jazz and blues and so, although he knew his father would never have approved, he opened a tavern where colored musicians could play jazz and the blues to their hearts' content. He met a woman and got married, but his wife never wanted children. She was too busy impressing the other women with her pretty clothes and lovely home. And, quite frankly, she felt that pregnancy would ruin her figure. Arnie could not say he had been happy in his marriage. His wife was impressively beautiful, but she was vain and self-absorbed.

Over the years, he had a couple of heartbreaking affairs with colored blues singers who'd stolen his heart when they performed at his establishment. He had even considered divorcing his wife and marrying one, but he didn't have the guts to go against society and that was what he would have had to do if he married a woman of color. He knew that. And so he finally stopped trying to be happy and accepted his life for what it was. By the time his wife passed away, his sexual desires had dwindled considerably. He put all of his energy into his work. However, lately he'd been feeling weak. He decided to ask Dovid if he wanted to take Arnie's car home with him at night and pick Arnie up at his house the following day He liked Dovid. Dovid was trustworthy and he felt like Dovid was the son he wished he had.

"You will be my driver, Dovid. Of course, you'll still be my bartender, and I will pay you a little bit extra for driving me. Then at night and on Sunday, you can use the car to take your wife out, or go wherever you need to go. All you have to do is make sure I have a ride back and forth to the tavern and you'll have to take care of all of my food shopping and whatever other errands I need you to run for me."

"Sure, Arnie," Dovid said. "But I have to get a driver's license first."

"You don't have one?"

"Not yet."

51

"You drove to pick Cool Breeze up at the flophouse a few months ago?"

"Yes, you asked me to do it so I did."

Arnie burst out laughing. "You sure have chutzpah!"

"I'll get a license."

"Take the afternoon off and go and get it today," Arnie said.

"Should I take the car?" Dovid asked.

Arnie laughed again. "Only if you want to be arrested. You can't drive to motor vehicles to get a license to drive. You are not supposed to be driving at all until you have the license."

Dovid shrugged his shoulders. "It's like a frozen wasteland out there today. Back in the old country we would have said it's like Siberia! After the snowstorm last night the temperature warmed up a little and the snow melted. Then this morning when the temperature dropped all the melted snow froze. Now the whole ground is solid ice. Ah…well… what can I do? I'll go to the bus stop and take the bus to get the license. By the way, do you have any idea where I should be going for this?"

"Yeah, of course. You gotta go to the department of motor vehicles. But, what the hell, why don't I just drive you?" Arnie said. "Cool Breeze can watch the place."

"That would be a lot better for me than standing at a bus stop in this weather," Dovid said.

Arnie called out to the back room where Cool Breeze was gathering cases of whiskey to stack behind the bar. "Hey Breeze, I have to take Dovi to pick something up, can you handle it while we're gone?"

"Surem, Mr. Arnie. I'm just stocking the bar for tonight," Cool Breeze said.

"We'll be back early, way before it gets busy," Arnie said.

CHAPTER TEN

Dovid got his driver's license and from that day on he was Arnie's driver. He picked him up in the afternoon and took him back home in the morning. They decided that on Wednesdays, Dovid would pick Arnie up early and they would go to the butcher, the bakery, and the market where Arnie would buy plenty of food to have in the house for the entire week.

That Sunday, Dovid, Harry, Eidel, and Ida took the car and went to Taylor Street for lunch. Then Dovid drove to the hockey game. It was a frigid day outside and there were still blankets of snow on the ground because it had snowed all day on Saturday. Dovid drove slowly because it was slippery and it was hard to keep control of the vehicle. However, he was glad that the couples didn't have to stand at a bus stop. Dovid smiled to himself as he thought, *We are very fortunate. We are riding in a heated automobile courtesy of Arnie Glassman. God bless you, Glassman.*

Neither of the wives had ever been to Taylor Street, better known as Little Italy. They looked around, eager to see the little neighborhood built by Italian immigrants.

"You know this Italian neighborhood is not so different from our little Jewish neighborhood? Jews? Italians? I guess in the long run all immigrants to this country are the same. We all come here to America with the same hopes and dreams," Ida said as she looked out the car window.

They stopped at a small restaurant where they enjoyed wonderful Italian beef sandwiches on thick rolls with sweet peppers. As they sat in the small neighborhood restaurant they looked out the window.

"You're right, Ida, it's not so different here than where we live," Dovid said.

"Except for the big Catholic Church across the street. Would you just look at that? The Catholics spent a fortune to build a fancy church, yet most of the Italian immigrants are struggling to survive. I am not sure how much they give to the church but I know that the church members give a part of their earnings to the church. The church doesn't care about the people," Harry said.

Eidel felt her face grow red. It bothered her to hear Harry speak ill of the Catholic church. Dovid glanced at Eidel quickly. He knew that her feelings had been hurt and he had to speak quickly. He had to put Harry in his place, but gently, before Eidel said something to Harry that would be very offensive.

"Harry, is it so different with a Jewish synagogue? We joined the temple and I can tell you this, it costs a fortune to be a member. And most of the Jewish immigrants can't afford it, either. It's the same thing as the Catholics. There is no difference," Dovid said. "You know when I got here to America, I was so excited to be able to be a practicing Jew. And don't get me wrong, I am proud of my heritage, but I don't know if I believe in religion."

"What does that mean, you don't believe in religion?"

"Just what I said. I think religion causes wars and hatred between people. I sometimes feel like I am Jewish by nationality, not because I follow the religion. However, religion isn't the only thing that causes people to hate each other. Coming to the U.S., I learned that race plays a big part in all of this, too. Just look at how people treat colored folks. The coloreds suffer for no reason other than the color of their skin. You know what I have learned as I have gotten older?"

"What?" Harry asked.

"I've learned that all people are really the same. We all really want and need the same things. Of course, food and shelter but also love, warmth, safety, and nice things for our families. And …we all bleed red blood," Dovid said.

"Well said, Dovi," Harry said smiling. "I think maybe you're right. Is that why you stopped wearing your yamulke?"

"I stopped wearing it because it was tearing my hair out. And I'm losing my hair fast enough as it is," Dovid laughed. "Listen, Harry, I am a Jew. My parents were Jews, I will always be a Jew. Hitler made sure that we knew that if we had a drop of Jewish blood we would always be Jews. And I want you to know that I am proud of being Jewish. But for me, what I am trying to say is that Judaism is more of a nationality than a religion. I work on Friday night and Saturday because I have to if I want to give my family a good life. I can't make my hours if I want to keep my job; I work when Arnie needs me. My parents kept kosher, but I don't keep kosher, as you can see …" Dovid indicated toward the Italian beef and French fries in front of him. "But whenever someone asks me what my background is, I tell them that the blood running through my veins is Jewish blood and I wouldn't have it any other way. I am proud to be a Jew even if I don't follow all the religious laws."

"That's why I like you, Dovi," Harry said.

They left the restaurant. Dovid opened the car door for Eidel. Harry opened the door to the backseat for his wife. They began the drive toward the stadium. In order to get there they had to drive through skid row where the restaurant Harry worked at was located. Harry was glad that it was cold, icy, and miserable outside because only half as many bums as usual were sleeping out on the street. The rest had found shelter. Still, even with the streets less littered with homeless men and prostitutes, Ida became worried about her husband's safety. She had never seen Harry's place of employment before.

"This is a very bad neighborhood. There are bars on the windows," Ida said. "And why are these people laying outside on the sidewalks?"

"They have no other place to go," Harry answered. He looked at Ida's face and realized that it had been a mistake to bring her there. She knew he worked in a rough area, but seeing it firsthand was different. He could see the shock in her eyes.

"Where is the restaurant where you work?"

"Oh, it's a couple of blocks down from here. The area gets better if you go down a little further," Harry lied.

Eidel turned back to look at Ida in the backseat. Ida shook her head. When she saw the concern in her friend's face, Eidel nodded to show Ida she agreed with her.

Their seats at the stadium were all the way upstairs in the bleachers, far from the ice. Once the players came out and the game started, Dovid and Harry tried to explain what was going on, but the girls weren't particularly interested in learning. They were talking amongst themselves as both teams glided across the ice.

"I must admit that I am impressed with their skating. But you boys keep telling me to keep my eye on the puck. The puck is so small and moves so fast that most of the time I have no idea where it is," Ida said, and everyone laughed.

They drank colas and sat huddled together because it was so cold in the stadium. The girls continued to chat softly, while the men cheered for the Blackhawks.

The Hawks lost two to three. Dovid and Harry were disappointed, but they really enjoyed the game. Both Eidel and Ida had a wonderful day. However, neither of them knew any more about hockey when they left the stadium as they did when they'd arrived.

The streetlights illuminated the frozen snow, giving the city the appearance of a winter wonderland.

"Maybe some night we can go to Chinatown and have dinner," Dovid said.

"Chinatown?" Ida asked.

"Yes," Harry said. "It's right near Little Italy."

"You know, it was really nice of that friend of yours to give you the tickets," Ida said to Harry.

"Yeah," Harry said.

"He just gave them to you?" Ida asked. "For no reason?"

"Yeah ..." Harry said. Then he changed the subject. "So, in the summer, let's all make plans to come downtown and look at the fountain."

"What fountain?" Eidel asked.

"Buckingham Fountain. It's really magnificent. The water changes colors," Harry answered.

"This city is amazing. There are some wonderful museums here, too. Now that I have access to a car we can go out more. We can explore Chicago," Dovid said.

"I would like that," Eidel took Dovid's hand.

"Are you warm enough?" he asked Eidel. "Or should I turn the heater higher?"

"I'm fine." She smiled at Dovid. Then she turned to the backseat "Are you two warm enough back there?"

"I am, are you?" Harry asked Ida.

"I am."

It's good to have access to an automobile. Arnie has his faults but I can't help but love him, Dovid thought as he turned the corner.

CHAPTER ELEVEN

When Dovid pulled the car up to Harry and Ida's apartment building to let them out there were two police cars with their lights flashing, blocking the entrance.

"I wonder what's going on here?" Ida said.

"Let's mind our own business," Harry answered. "Thank you for driving us tonight, Dovi. We'll see you both for dinner next week? It's our turn, so you'll come at six on Sunday?"

"Of course," Dovid said.

"I'll call you tomorrow," Ida said to Eidel.

Eidel nodded.

Harry and Ida got out of the car and began to head up the walkway to their building when two police officers came up from behind and grabbed Harry.

Dovid couldn't hear the conversation between Harry and the officer, but he saw what happened. He put the car in park. "You stay here. I'll be right back. This has to be a misunderstanding," Dovid said to Eidel. He jumped out but left the car running with the heat on. Then he ran over to where Harry and Ida were standing, both of them looking dumbfounded.

"Hey, what's going on here, officer?" Dovid said.

"This is none of your business," the cop said to Dovid.

"It is my business. This man is my best friend."

"He has to come down to the station with us for questioning. He is under investigation for murder."

"Murder? Are you crazy? I know this man, he could never kill anyone."

"We'll be the judge of that," the cop said to Dovid, then he turned to Harry and said "Let's go. You can go on upstairs, Mrs. Rosen. We'll be in touch."

The officers pushed Harry into the back of the police car. Dovid's eyes caught Harry's. Harry shrugged as if he had no idea why all of this was happening. But Dovid could see the fear in his friend's face. He turned to Ida. "Wait here for a minute," Dovid said. Then he ran back to the car. He opened the door on the passenger's side.

"What is it? What's happening?" Eidel asked.

"Something is going on here with Harry. I don't know what it is. It's all very confusing. You go inside and stay with Ida. I am going to take a ride down to the police station and see if I can help Harry to get this all straightened out."

"What do they want with Harry?" Eidel asked.

"They are saying they want to question him about a murder. I know it's all a mistake. They have the wrong man. That's all it is. I am sure of it. Go upstairs with Ida. Let me handle this. I'll call you here at Harry's apartment as soon as I have a better idea of what's happening."

"This is very scary, Dovi."

"Don't be afraid. Let me handle everything." Dovid kissed his wife and helped her out of the automobile then walked her up the walkway to where Ida stood shivering in the cold wind. "I'm going to the police station. Eidel will stay with you."

Ida nodded. Eidel put her arm around her friend's shoulder and the two women walked up three stairs to the door of the apartment building. Dovid followed them and then he watched from the bottom floor until they were safely inside the Rosens' apartment. Once the door closed and locked, he raced back to the automobile and drove straight to the police station.

CHAPTER TWELVE

Harry looked small sitting on a bench. Dovid was not permitted to talk to him. So Dovid went to the police officer in charge.

"I demand to know why you have arrested my friend."

"This doesn't concern you," the officer said. "Go home."

Dovid knew only one man with enough influence to get information from the police. Arnie Glassman. Dovi knew that Arnie paid off plenty for the cops to overlook things that happened at the tavern. Over the years, a man who earned the kind of money that Arnie did earned respect. If Dovid could get Arnie to help him, the police might give him more information. Information he could use to help Harry. But, Arnie was Dovid's boss. Never once had Dovid asked Arnie for a favor. He was always on time for work and did whatever Arnie asked. Since he'd been hired, Dovid was grateful to have his job and he hated to put it in jeopardy by waking his boss in the middle of the night to ask for help with a police matter. Yet, how could he walk out and just leave Harry sitting there on the bench?

Dovid walked over to the public phone. He searched his pocket for a dime to call Arnie. As he was scanning his pocket for change, Mike Marshall and his sister Sharon Burns, along with her husband Clem, came rushing into the police station. Sharon's face was tear-stained and Mike looked furious. Clem was hanging back with his arms wrapped around his chest.

He looked like a frightened dog waiting for instructions from a cruel master.

"My son! My Ralph was killed," Dovid heard Sharon say. "That man is responsible. I know it. I am sure of it. As sure as I'm standing here. You see Ralphy took his hours at work and because of it I know that Harry Rosen hated my boy." Sharon Burns was ranting at the police.

Dovid walked away from the phone to listen. Sharon was screaming so loud that everyone in the station could hear her.

"Didn't you hate Ralph, Harry? He took money out of your pocket, food out of your mouth. So, you set him up, didn't you? Don't lie…"

Harry shook his head. "NO, never! I don't know what you're talking about. I would never do such a terrible thing."

"It's all so fucking obvious, Harry. You were supposed to work tonight but you arranged to take tonight off. You asked Ralph to work for you. You knew that he would be killed tonight. Come on Harry; admit it. This didn't happen by chance. You wanted to get rid of Ralph so you set the whole thing up to look like a robbery. You sent some bum into the restaurant tonight to rob the place and get rid of my son, my only son." Sharon began crying again. "My Ralphy, such a young boy, so much potential. Because of you, Harry Rosen, he was ripped from this earth in the prime of his life."

"I swear to you, I had nothing to do with it. Nothing," Harry said. "I would never do a thing like that."

"Why did you take off tonight?" the police officer asked.

"I got tickets for a hockey game. My wife and I went to see the game with our friends."

"Hockey tickets? You bought hockey tickets? You must have plenty of spare cash. Mr. Marshall must pay you well." The officer pushed back his hair with his hand.

"I got the tickets as a gift."

"Oh, sure, somebody just gave you tickets to a Blackhawks game. Is that right? Is that what you're telling me?"

"One of the bus drivers who worked at the Grayline next door had tickets. He's a friend of mine. He gave them to me."

"I see. And he just gave them to you? As a gift?"

"No, he gave them to me because I did him a favor."

"What kind of a favor, Mr. Rosen?"

Harry was trembling. Because of the time he'd spent at Auschwitz he got nervous when he was questioned by anyone in authority or anyone in a uniform.

Harry Rosen cleared his throat. His face was a ghostly gray. "The fellow asked me to cover for him in case his boss came looking for him."

"I don't understand. I think you had better explain," the officer said.

"Yeah, I think so," Mike Marshall chimed in, nodding his head.

"As you know, the Grayline bus station is right next door to the restaurant. A lot of the drivers come in to eat before or after their shift. This driver was late to start his route one night..."

"Why is that? What was this man doing that made him late?"

Harry looked at Dovi across the room. Dovi could see the fear in Harry's face. He walked over to where the conversation was taking place. "My name is Dovid Levi. I am Harry Rosen's best friend. I can tell you that he is a man of good character."

"Nobody asked you," Mike Marshall said.

"I was with him at the game tonight. Our wives were with us too."

"That doesn't mean he didn't set Ralphy up."

"I know he didn't," Dovid said.

"You know this for a fact?"

Dovid could not say that he did know it for certain. So he just looked at Harry. "Tell them everything, Harry."

"Yes, Harry, tell us everything. What was the driver doing that you had to cover for him?"

"He went upstairs to a room with a hooker. I knew about it because I rented the room to him for an hour. He came back two hours later. I didn't charge him for the extra time and he was late to start his route. When his boss came in for coffee the following morning and asked me what happened, I said that the driver was sick in the bathroom," Harry said. "The driver was a nice fellow, I didn't want to see him lose his job. So, I lied for him."

"Well, if you would lie for him then who's to say you aren't just a liar in general?" Mike Marshall said. "I'm disappointed in you, Harry. Very disappointed."

"But I swear to you, there was no set up to hurt Ralph," Harry said.

"We need to investigate this further," the police officer said to everyone. Then he turned to Harry. "You'll be our guest for the night here at the station," he added.

"But I have done nothing wrong," Harry said, almost ready to cry. "There have been robberies at the restaurant when I was working. I don't know why this man killed Ralph. All I know is that I had nothing to do with it."

"I suggest you tell Mrs. Rosen it would be a good idea if her husband got a lawyer," the policeman said to Dovid.

"A lawyer?"

"Yeah."

Harry looked at Dovid and Dovid could see how frightened Harry was as they took Harry to lock him behind bars.

"Don't worry, Harry, I'll help you, "Dovid said.

Before he left the police station, Dovid went to the public phone and called Arnie. From the way Arnie sounded when he said hello, Dovid knew that he'd awakened him out of a deep sleep. "Arnie, it's Dovi. I need help."

Without hesitation, and without asking a single question Arnie said, "Sure, kid. Get yourself over here to my house right now. I'll throw on a pot of coffee and you can tell me what you need."

"I'll be right over," Dovid said.

By the time Dovid arrived at Arnie's house it was a quarter to two in the morning. Arnie was sitting at the kitchen table in his boxer shorts, sipping a cup of black coffee.

"Get yourself a cup of coffee then sit down and tell me

what the hell is going on," Arnie said.

Dovid told Arnie all that he knew.

"What do you think, Dovi? Do you believe Harry was involved?"

"One hundred percent no," Dovid said. "He would never do such a thing. I know Harry."

"Did he ever tell you that he resented the kid for taking his hours?"

"Yeah, he probably did. But Harry would never get involved in the taking of a life. I am telling you. I know this for sure."

"I trust you, Dovi. I believe in you. You've been like a son to me. You know that, don't you?"

"You've been like a Papa to me. Before I met you, Arnie, I thought I was alone in the world. Both my parents are dead. They died when I was just a kid. You were the closest thing I've had to a parent," Dovid said.

"What happened to them? You know, you never told me."

Dovid took a sip of the hot coffee. Then he told Arnie everything about his past, all about Babi Yar and fighting in the Russian army. He told him how ashamed he was for hiding his Jewish identity and living as a non-Jew for so many years. Arnie listened, then he nodded.

"You did what you had to do to survive, kid. I don't blame you one bit. I woulda done the same thing," Arnie said. "Now that I know what we have to do, why don't you go home and get some rest? As soon as the sun comes up I'll call my lawyer, Fred Lichtenstien. I don't know if you've ever met Fred, but he is a really sharp lawyer. He'll know what we have to do. He's gotten me out of plenty of messes. That's why I keep him on retainer."

"I think I met him once. A short guy, wiry gray hair? About fifty?"

"That's him."

"He came to see you at the tavern when I was working. It was a long time ago. But I remembered that he said he was your lawyer."

"Yeah, he comes in once in a while. Most of the time, when I have business with him, he comes to my house. Anyway, I'll call him at the crack of dawn. Then all three of us will go down to the police station and get this thing straightened out for your friend."

"Arnie ... I can't thank you enough," Dovid said.

"Yeah, yeah, don't worry about it. Pick me up at eight. And bring some bagels from the deli on the corner, cream cheese, too. You got it?"

"Yes, Arnie. You want a salt bagel, right?"

"You know it kid. And, hey, don't worry. We'll get this all fixed up. I've had to take care of a lot of worse things in my time," Arnie said, patting Dovid's shoulder.

CHAPTER THIRTEEN

Dovid went to Ida's apartment to pick up his wife but Eidel refused to leave Ida alone. Dovid told the women what Arnie was going to do in the morning, then he laid down on the couch. He was exhausted, but his mind was still going a hundred miles an hour. Harry, his best friend, was stuck behind bars.

At least an American jail is nothing compared to what Harry endured under the Nazis. But I've got a feeling that Harry is probably reliving some terrible memories tonight.

Dovid consoled himself with the fact that Arnie was a rich man and an influential man.

He has important people as friends; he has a good lawyer. I am very fortunate to have him as a friend. If anyone can help Harry, it's Arnie.

"If I fall asleep, please be sure to wake me up before six. The deli opens at seven. I have to pick up Arnie's breakfast on the way to his house."

"I'll make sure you're awake," Ida said. "And thank you for helping us. Please … I want you to know that I promise you that my Harry had nothing to do with this."

"Of course, we know that," Eidel said, putting her arm around her friend. "Why don't you try to get some rest? At least lie down."

Ida nodded and allowed Eidel to guide her to her bed. She

lay down and Eidel lay where Harry usually slept. The women were silent but neither fell asleep. They were both waiting for morning.

CHAPTER FOURTEEN

As Arnie had promised, Fred was magnificent. He took care of everything. And by noon the following day, Harry was released on a bond that Arnie paid.

"They have nothing on him," Fred said to Dovid. "Listen, they have a killer, they have a motive, but they have no proof of anything as far as Harry being involved. Don't worry about this situation. There isn't going to be a problem."

Harry thanked Arnie a hundred times. He thanked Dovid too. Ida hugged her husband, then she hugged Arnie, Dovid, and Fred, tears running down her cheeks.

"Well, I have to get to court. I'll see to it that this whole thing disappears," Fred said to Arnie.

"I owe you," Arnie said.

"Don't mention it …" Fred said. Then he tipped his hat, winked, and left.

"Dovi, let's drop the girls at home, take Harry to the restaurant, and then get our asses in to work."

Dovid nodded. "Thank you from the bottom of my heart, Arnie."

"Stop with all the sentimental bullshit. We have a business to run," Arnie said. But Dovid could see in Arnie's eyes that he was glad he had been able to help.

Eidel put her arm around Ida and Dovid patted Harry's

shoulder. "Let's go," Dovid said.

CHAPTER FIFTEEN

Arnie had his faults; he could be stubborn and racist. But Dovid loved him regardless. To Dovid, Cool Breeze was and had always been an equal. But he knew that Arnie didn't feel the same way. Dovid knew from Cool Breeze that Arnie had been seriously involved with at least two colored women. It was something they never discussed. Dovi wondered if maybe they had broken Arnie's heart. Still, Dovid knew better than to ask. But if Arnie had any shortcomings, it was his views on colored people.

A famous blues singer was coming to Chicago. May Allen Davis. She had made surprise appearances at the tavern in the past. Arnie was hoping that she would show up when she was in town.

"The last time she came the crowd went wild," Arnie told Dovid.

"I wasn't here yet."

"No, it was before I hired you. Look at this picture." Arnie showed Dovid the picture on May's album cover. He looked at the woman. She was tall and slender with skin the color of cream with just a touch of coffee. Her hair was elegantly processed, leaving it finger-waved perfectly around her lovely face. May wore an ivory floor-length gown and held a single red rose in one hand.

"You met May Allen Davis, didn't you Cool Breeze?"

"Yes, Mr. Arnie, I sure did. She is a real lady."

"You wanna hear her voice?" Arnie asked Dovid.

"Sure."

"Go put the record on. Turn it up loud so we all can hear," Arnie said.

Dovid placed the riveted black record on the turntable. Then he carefully placed the arm with the needle at the end of the vinyl circle, turning the knob to increase the volume to its full capacity. The record began to play and the sweet sound of a magical soprano voice filled with depth of feeling touched Dovid deep inside the pit of his stomach.

After the first song was over, Dovid turned to Cool Breeze. "She's good."

"Sounds a little like Billy Holiday, don't she?"

"Yes, she certainly does."

"You know, Arnie gots it bad for her. Last time she come here, she went home with him. Probably she spent the night at his house," Cool Breeze whispered to Dovid.

CHAPTER SIXTEEN

Dovid arrived home from work that night. He was tired and hungry but when he sat down to eat he saw that Eidel was pale.

"Are you feeling all right? You're going to have a baby; you should be getting plenty of rest. Have you talked to a doctor about what to do when you're pregnant?" Dovid was worried about Eidel. She was delicate in mind and body and he knew that. He also knew that she hadn't gotten much sleep the night before because of Harry but he had figured she would sleep all day and be fine by the time he got home. But she didn't look fine. She looked drained.

"You should have called me at work and told me you were tired. You didn't have to cook. I would have picked something up on the way home and let you sleep. I wish you would have slept instead of cooking." He got up and felt her forehead for fever.

"Dovi, I'm fine. But Harry isn't. Ida and I have been on the phone all day. Harry got fired today. Ida is sick about it. They have a little bit of money saved but not much. I don't know what they are going to do."

"All right, Eidel. It will be all right. Don't worry about anything. You just try to get some rest. Let me take care of this."

"You've always taken care of everything, Dovi. I don't know what I would do without you."

"Well, don't even think about that. You worry yourself sick constantly. You're going to have a baby. You need to stay calm. Please, relax and let me see what I can do."

"You and I both know that Harry and Ida won't take any help from us."

"They will if they need it badly enough. Now, please, I am begging you to just stop worrying. Let me think about this whole thing and see what I can come up with."

Dovid ate quickly then he took Eidel to their room and tucked her into bed. "Sleep....you need your rest. You're going to be a mother." He kissed her forehead. Then he lay down beside her, an idea about Harry was already forming in his mind.

CHAPTER SEVENTEEN

The following day, even though it was three in the afternoon, Dovid stopped at the deli and picked up a salt bagel with cream cheese for Arnie on his way over to pick him up. He got a plain bagel for himself. Arnie was pleasantly surprised. "Nice gesture, Levi." He smiled as he unwrapped his snack. "We're not in a hurry. Let's sit down at the table like mensch and eat. We have a little time. Let's enjoy our food instead of eating while we drive, huh?" Arnie said, unwrapping his sandwich.

Dovid knew that Arnie would want to sit down at the table and take a little time to eat in peace. He had to talk to Arnie and this was just the opportunity Dovid had hoped for

They sat at Arnie's kitchen table. "Want a cola?" Arnie asked. "Or do you want to put up a pot of coffee?"

"Up to you," Dovid said.

"Get a couple of bottles of pop from the refrigerator. I have grape soda, cola, orange. Take what you want. Get me a cola," Arnie said and sat down. "The bottle opener is in the drawer," Arnie pointed.

Dovid put the open soda in front of Arnie and another in front of himself. Then he sat down across from Arnie and began to eat.

"Nu? So what's on your mind, kid?" Arnie said.

"How do you know something is on my mind?" Dovid

asked.

"Come on Dovi, I know you. You planned this whole late lunch so we could talk. Come on. Out with it."

"Harry got canned last night. He has no job."

"I don't have an opening at the bar for him. You know that. We don't need any help."

"I know that. But I have an idea," Dovid said. "This idea I have ... it would be good for him, but it would be great for you. You'd make even more money and you'd be helping Harry at the same time."

"Come on, boy genius. Tell me already. You drag everything out."

"Okay, okay. So here goes. Why don't we put a snack bar in the tavern? A small restaurant. Nothing fancy. Sandwiches, hamburgers, Vienna hot dogs, French fries. People will love it and they'll stay longer, which means that they'll drink more. Harry could run the snack bar. He has plenty of experience. I know he didn't cook for Mike, but he can. Nu? What do you think?"

For a moment, Arnie was silent then a smile spread across his face reaching all the way up to his eyes. "That's what I love about you, boychick. You got the smarts, and you're always thinking."

"You like the idea?"

"I love it. Call Harry. Let's get this thing going with him."

CHAPTER EIGHTEEN

Harry and Cool Breeze put the snack bar together. Cool Breeze built out an area set in the back of the dance floor where a patron could come up to the counter and order food. Harry used the connections he'd worked with at Mike's to order food wholesale at a reasonable rate. Within two weeks, the snack bar was up and running. The food was sensibly priced, making it an instant success. It was even a good addition for Dovid, Cool Breeze, Harry, and Arnie, as they no longer had to go out to purchase food if they got hungry during their work shift.

May Allen Davis did surprise everyone and make an appearance at the tavern one night, wearing a full-length red satin gown. Within minutes of her arrival she was surrounded by fans. They coaxed her up to the microphone where she sang two songs with the resident piano player accompanying. Arnie sent over a round of free drinks for her and the entourage she'd brought along. Then he went over to May and put his hand on her shoulder. From where Dovid was standing behind the bar, he could see that there was chemistry between Arnie and May. But he couldn't hear what they were saying. Then Arnie took May's hand. May stood up and the two began to slow dance as the piano played softly in the background.

That night when it was time to leave, Arnie told Dovid to go on home without him.

"How are you going to get home?" Dovid asked.

"I'll be here at the bar tomorrow. Don't worry about picking me up. I'll be just fine," Arnie said.

Dovid was puzzled until he saw Arnie leave with his arm around May.

He's going to a hotel with her. Arnie is such a strange man.

Dovid thought about Arnie as he drove home after his shift was over.

I love him like a father, but he confuses me. He has such strange and conflicting views about race and religion.

CHAPTER NINETEEN

At the end of August, at four o'clock in the morning, Eidel went into labor. When she touched Dovid's shoulder to let him know that it was time, he jumped out of bed. He dressed quickly and drove her to Mount Sinai Hospital. Once Eidel was taken to her room, Dovid called Arnie and told him that he would not be in to work the following day because Eidel was in labor. Within an hour, Arnie arrived at the hospital; he'd taken a taxi. He found Dovid and sat down beside him in the waiting room.

"I should probably call Ida. Eidel would want her to know," Dovid said.

"She probably already knows. I called Harry and told him that we wouldn't be in to work today, then I told him to tell Cool Breeze."

Ida arrived at noon. She'd taken the bus.

"You want something to eat?" Arnie asked Dovid and Ida. Both of them declined, so Arnie sat back down and waited. After fifteen hours of hard labor, the doctor decided it was necessary to do a cesarean section.

Arnie and Ida sat in the waiting room with Dovid, who was a nervous wreck. He couldn't eat and was having a hard time sitting still.

"A cesarean section means they have to cut her," Dovid said. "My God, Eidel. She must be so scared. I want to get in there and see her."

"Calm down Dovi. She'll be all right," Arnie said, placing his hand on Dovid's shoulder.

Ida just sat stone-faced, staring out the window.

Cool Breeze and Harry took care of everything at the tavern. They called several times the following day to see how Eidel was doing.

Dovid was too distressed to take their calls, so Arnie talked to them.

"I am worried sick about her," Dovid said.

"I know, Dovi. But she's going to be fine. You'll see." Arnie patted Dovid's shoulder.

Ida sat wringing her hands. She didn't speak to either of the men. She seemed lost in her own world of worry. Her eyes seemed to say, "A woman can easily die in childbirth."

"The cutting is bothering me," Dovid said, breaking a long silence. "When they cut there is a greater chance of infection."

"Your father was a doctor, wasn't he?"

"Yes," Dovid said. "I saw him deliver babies. And plenty of women died."

"Well don't even think about anything going wrong. It won't," Arnie declared. trying to sound confident. "She has a good doctor. I know Doctor Silverman personally. He is a good friend of mine. He knows that you are like a son to me. He'll take good care of Eidel. She is going to be just fine."

Dovid knew Arnie was right about the obstetrician. After all, Arnie had hired and paid Dr. Silverman to handle all the details of the pregnancy of Eidel Levi.

Finally, after what seemed like a lifetime, Dr. Silverman came into the waiting room.

"You have a son. A healthy baby boy. Mrs. Levi is doing fine. Congratulations," Dr. Silverman said. He shook David's hand. Then he shook Arnie's hand.

"Good job, Doc," Arnie said, patting the doctor's shoulder.

The doctor smiled. "Give her a few minutes. Then you can all go in and see her."

"Thank you, Doctor," Dovid said.

Dovid happened to glance over and catch a glimpse of Ida's eyes. In them, he saw the relief that he felt.

When they all went into the room, Eidel was sitting up holding the baby. Her hair was spread like silk across the pillow. She smiled at Dovid and he thought she looked like an angel.

"You are so beautiful," Dovid said, leaning down to kiss Eidel.

"Meet your son," she smiled.

Dovid looked down into the blanket. His heart swelled. "Oy, what a mitzvah...he's really something," Dovid said, touching the baby's cheek.

"A boy, Dovid. What nachas, what good luck!" Arnie said. "So since I am like his grandfather, I'll pay to make the bris."

"I don't want to hear about the bris right now," Eidel joked. "What mother wants to hear about the big party everyone is planning for her tiny infant son's circumcision?"

"That's why we never let the mother in the room when the moyel does the cutting," Arnie said.

"Stop, please…" Eidel said. Then she smiled and said to Dovid, "He is a marvel, a true gift from God, isn't he?"

"He is. He really is," Dovid said.

"Since the Jewish name their children for their dead loved ones, I would like to name him for my father, Menachem," Dovid said. "We only need to use the first letter of my Papa's name." Eidel wanted to name their first child after Helen, but she knew how much it meant to Dovid that he gave his father a namesake and so she agreed to name the little boy Mark Joseph Levi, after Dovid's father Menachem Jacob Levi.

"You didn't put the nursery together, I hope," Arnie said.

"No, I couldn't. It's considered bad luck in the Jewish religion to put a nursery together before a baby is born. Now I have to hurry up and get everything ready before Eidel and the baby come home."

"You did it right," Arnie said smiling. "But it looks like you and I have some work to do Dovi," Arnie said.

Dovid and Arnie left right away in order to set up the nursery.

"I'll stay here with Eidel until you get back. Then maybe you can drive me home when you leave?" Ida asked Dovid.

"Of course. But are you sure you want to stay here all day?"

"I'm sure."

Arnie insisted upon buying the baby's crib. And while he was having fun playing grandfather, he also bought a high chair and a bag of infant clothes.

Since Dovid and Eidel lived in a small apartment with only

one bedroom, the living room became the nursery. Once everything was set up, Dovid and Arnie went out to a deli to grab a sandwich before they headed back to the hospital.

The restaurant had red-checked tablecloths and a loud waitress who yelled orders at the man who was slicing the deli meat.

Dovid and Arnie got a table by the window. They both ordered corned beef on rye.

"I can't thank you enough for everything you have done for me," Dovid said. "You are such a blessing to me and my family."

"Echh. Come on. We're friends. What are friends for?"

"You're not just a friend, you're a good friend, Arnie."

"Yeah, I try to be. You may not realize this, but you have done as much for me as I've done for you."

"How is that possible? What do you mean?"

"I mean you gave me a family … a sense of purpose. I have always had plenty of money but I never had anyone care about me. I believe you do, Dovi."

"Cool Breeze cares about you, too."

"But I told you, coloreds are different."

"I don't buy that, Arnie. In fact, I don't even believe that you believe that."

"They have drug and alcohol problems."

"You mean to tell me that a white person can't have those problems?"

"Of course they can. But more of the coloreds have

addictions. I'm not saying all of them. But a lot of them. Most of the ones we come in contact with anyway."

"You want to know why?"

"Sure, boy genius. Why?"

"Because there are white pushers out there who use the fact that the coloreds are made to feel inferior. They know how hard it is to be a colored person. Colored people can't get good jobs and don't get paid as much as whites. So these white pushers introduce them to heroin with all kinds of promises. They lie to them and tell them that the drugs will take away their pain. The pushers want to get them hooked. So, they do whatever it takes to get them started on heroin so they can suck money out of them forever."

"Yeah, sounds about right," Arnie said. "It's a pity. A fellow like Cool Breeze has so much talent and intelligence. But it's just a matter of time before he slips and goes back on the needle. That's the way it is with heroin."

"Can we send him to a clinic or do something to help him? I'd be willing to help with the financial aspect even if it meant taking a drastic cut in pay," Dovid asked.

"Not that I know of, boychick. I'm sorry. I really am, because I like him. In fact, I am going to tell you a secret that I don't normally tell anyone."

"Go on, you know you can trust me, Arnie."

"Well, Dovi, in my lifetime, I have actually fallen in love with colored women. Don't look so shocked."

"I'm not shocked. I always knew that you didn't really believe that they were less than us because of the color of their skin."

"I never said less, Dovid. I said different. They are different because of their background. Their ancestors were slaves in this country. And there are a lot of assholes in the south who still treat them like they should be slaves."

"I remember you once said to me that you paid Cool Breeze well for a colored man. I never understood how a man as good and kind as you could say something so small-minded."

"You're right. It is small-minded of me. But you don't understand why I do it. I make sure Breeze has whatever he needs. But I don't pay him what he deserves, not because he's colored but because I'm afraid he'll spend his money on drugs and alcohol."

"But it's his money. He works for it. Shouldn't he have the right to do with it whatever he chooses?"

"That works in theory. But when it comes down to the real world, Dovi, sometimes you have to protect a person from themselves."

Dovid thought about what Arnie had just said. He didn't agree. But he wouldn't argue with Arnie, either. Dovid was sure that there had to be someone who could help Cool Breeze get straightened out—a doctor, a clinic, someone? He would have to look into it further as soon as he had a chance. Right now, he was overwhelmed with his own new responsibilities. He, Dovid Levi, was a father. They finished their sandwiches.

"Let's get back to the hospital," Arnie said.

CHAPTER TWENTY

November arrived and with it came an early winter storm. It brought a rain of soft snow that made driving difficult. But the worst of it was that Cool Breeze disappeared the second week of November. For six nights he didn't show up at the bar. Dovid drove to the flophouse and went up to room 402 to look for him, but when he knocked another man opened the door. Not knowing what else to do, Dovid went to the restaurant where he'd met Harry and asked the new man whom Mike had hired if he could help him locate Crawford B. Dell. The man was short with him. He said he'd never heard of a Crawford B. Dell. "This is a flophouse, we don't have a sign-in register. I have no idea of the names of the people who come and go here. After all, we rent by the hour. Could you imagine if I tried to keep track of all of these bums?" Mike's new employee said.

Onefeather was standing at the grill. Dovid gave the tall Native American man a pleading look. He knew that Onefeather would recognize him.

"I'm sorry," Onefeather said, shrugging his shoulders. "I haven't seen Cool Breeze in here since Harry left. He might have moved on to one of the other flop houses down the street."

There was nothing to do but wait and hope that Cool Breeze would return. Arnie and Dovid were distraught. They were both afraid that something terrible had happened but neither said a word. Then, the first week in December, as if he'd never been gone, Cool Breeze returned with a big smile on his face.

"How you all been?" he asked.

"I ought to fire you," Arnie said, shaking his head. His face was red with anger.

"You ought to but you won't," Cool Breeze said.

"We were worried," Dovid said as he wiped down the bar. "We didn't know if you were dead or alive."

"Well, here I is; just as alive as you."

"Maybe you should go and check into a hospital and get straightened out," Dovid said.

"Awe shit. Come on now, I am fine. I had me a good time with a beautiful lady. Cost me a small fortune. Everything I had. But believe you me; she was worth every penny. I tell you, every woman's sittin' on a gold mine. Ain't that the truth," Cool Breeze said and laughed.

Dovid was so angry at Cool Breeze that he wanted to punch him. But at the same time, he was so damn glad to see him that he put his arms around Breeze and gave him a bear hug.

CHAPTER TWENTY-ONE

Later that same month, Dovid was pouring a whiskey when he heard two gunshots. He turned in the direction from which they came. Two men and a woman were standing on the dance floor; the rest of the customers had cleared out.

"Get down, Harry," Dovid yelled. Harry ducked. Cool Breeze and Dovid knelt down on the pallets behind the bar.

"Stay in the back," Dovid yelled to Arnie. "Somebody is shooting out here. Can you hear me, Arnie?"

Arnie didn't answer. "Call the police, Arnie," Harry yelled.

There was still no answer. But one of the customers must have gone to the phone and called. The phone booth was right outside of the entrance to the L station next to Comisky Park, which was not even a block away.

The gun fired again. Dovid couldn't see anything over the bar, so he had no idea if someone had been shot or if the gunman was just shooting into the air to scare his victim. There was a lot of yelling. Dovid and Cool Breeze were together and they stayed down. But Harry and Arnie were both alone—Harry was behind the snack bar and Arnie was in the back room.

"Don't move, Mister Dovi. Stay still, stay quiet," Cool Breeze whispered.

"I hope Arnie doesn't come out," Dovid said.

"Don't you worry about Mister Arnie. He knows better

than to come out during a gunfight. That's why he didn't answer you. He don't want them that's fightin' to know where he is. Just in case they got the notion that since they had the gun anyway, they ought to rob the joint," Cool Breeze whispered.

Dovid felt a gush of relief come over him as he heard the loud sirens of the police cars. *Thank God this would soon be over.*

Four policemen came rushing in with their guns drawn. The customer who had been firing the weapon was very drunk and angry. He was waving the pistol in the air.

"Drop the gun," the officer said. The gunman was ranting that the man he'd been fighting with had slept with his wife. He fired another shot; this time it broke the window.

"Drop the weapon," the officer said, his voice threatening. "Drop it now, or I am going to shoot you."

The man fired another shot. The officer shot him in the arm and the gun fell from his hand. The cop grabbed the gun.

Blood ran from the shooter's arm. The police handcuffed both of the men involved and took them away.

"Who's in charge here? We need to take a statement," one of the officers said.

"Arnie Glassman, the owner. He's in the back room," Dovid said.

"Arnie Glassman, come out to the front," the cop said. But there was no answer.

"Can I go back and get him?" Dovid asked.

"Yeah, go on."

Dovid walked in the back to the storage area where he saw

Arnie on the floor. Arnie must have been lifting a box of whiskey bottles when he keeled over. He lay on the ground with his hand on his chest and all of the bottles scattered around him, the floor sprinkled with shards of glass and whiskey. Dovid raced over to embrace his friend but he knew, even before he held Arnie gently in his arms, that Arnie was gone. Dovid sat on the floor and wept quietly as he held Arnie, rocking him like a baby. Dovid could hardly swallow, but he whispered to the body that was already small and empty of spirit, "Arnie, my God, I am going to miss you. I never expected you to go like this. Damn you, Arnie. You never gave me a chance to say goodbye." Tears were running down Dovid's face.

The police finally came into the room.

"What happened here?"

"I don't know," Dovid said. "I think he probably had a heart attack."

Cool Breeze and Harry came in and found Dovid still sitting in the middle of the floor with Arnie in his arms.

"Oh Jesus," Cool Breeze said. He sat down beside Dovid and put his arm around him. Breeze whispered, "We done lost a good friend tonight."

"Someone should call an ambulance," Harry said.

Dovid nodded, but he couldn't move. He couldn't put Arnie down on the floor.

"I'll make the call," Harry said.

"Don't worry about it. We'll call for an ambulance on the radio," the police officer said.

The lights, the noise, and the chaos in the emergency room were giving Dovid a terrible headache. He'd been getting migraines lately and now he was seeing spots from the glare.

"Was it a heart attack?" Cool Breeze asked the doctor.

"Yes, he had a massive heart attack. He died quickly. He didn't suffer," the doctor assured Dovid, Harry, and Cool Breeze.

"Put a sign outside the bar that we're closed until further notice," Dovid said. Then he turned and left the hospital to go home. The icy wind slapped his face and the reality of his loss that night set in.

Arnie. What am I going to do without you?

Harry and Cool Breeze were taking care of all of the arrangements. Harry even gave Cool Breeze a suit to wear to the funeral.

Dovid was at home sitting on the sofa just staring at the wall when Harry called him. He wanted to get some information so that he could put things together for Arnie's burial.

"Do you know if Arnie has purchased a plot somewhere?" Harry asked Dovid.

"I don't know," Dovid said. "He probably did. Check with Forest Lawn. His parents and his wife are all buried there."

"All right. I'll call them."

Harry found that Arnie had a prepaid plot with the rest of his family. While making the arrangements, he discovered that Arnie once had a stillborn son. The infant's grave was located right next to the headstones of Arnie's parents. But, oddly, its tiny gravestone read only, "Infant boy, Born and died 1949, Father, Arnie Glassman." There was no name for the mother. As far as Harry knew, Arnie had never mentioned this child to anyone. It made Harry wonder who was this unfortunate baby's mother, and why had Arnie kept this a secret? Harry decided that Dovid was too distraught right now to mention anything about this to him. Harry figured Dovid would see the little grave when they all went to bury Arnie at the cemetery.

If Dovid saw the child's grave, he never mentioned it to anyone. He stood rigid and frozen in grief as the casket was lowered into the ground. It was a gray and cloudy day, the cold wind whipped and an icy rain combined with tears across Dovid's face. Eidel stood beside her husband, not knowing what to do or say. She held his arm and squeezed it, trying to reassure him. But since he'd started working at this job, it was as if they'd grown apart. He was away at work more than he was at home. She hardly ever saw him anymore. Their relationship was polite but distant and Eidel no longer knew how to comfort him. She was silent as the rain drenched her clothes and hair.

Dovid was too distressed to do anything but grieve. He couldn't bear to talk to anyone. He went into his room and lay on his bed alone during the seven day Shiva. This was a time of mourning when the mourners sat on wooden boxes and wore black. The mirrors were covered and those who came to offer condolences brought food and made sure to eat something sweet before they left. The Shiva could have been at Arnie's house but Dovid insisted that they have it at his apartment. When Dovid tore the lapel of his shirt, as is the Jewish tradition to show that someone is in mourning, he felt as if his heart were being torn in two.

Even when Mark was crying, Dovid never came out of his bedroom to comfort his child. But he did come out for the minyan when the rabbi arranged for ten men to say prayers for the dead.

Dovid was too upset to even go down to the bar and put up a sign saying they would be closed for the next seven days. He asked Cool Breeze to do it for him.

After the Shiva was over, Harry insisted that Dovid get out of bed and get back to work.

"You can't stay in the house like this, laying in the bed in your room. It's not healthy and you are growing more depressed by the day. We have both known plenty of loss, Dovi. And because of this, we both know that the only way to survive is to get up and keep on going forward with our lives." .

"You're right," Dovid said. But it was difficult to find the strength to go on.

"Come on. You have to put on some clothes. We'll go in to the bar today."

Harry patted Dovid's shoulder. "Cool Breeze is staying with me at my apartment. I invited him to stay until the dust settled and we could get back to a normal life. So after you get ready we can go and pick him up."

"I can't believe I won't be going to Arnie's house this afternoon to pick him up. I wish to God I could bring him a salt bagel," Dovid said and tears formed at the corners of his eyes. "It's hard to accept that we won't see him again tonight. He was like a papa to me, Harry. He wasn't perfect. But who is? In his heart, Arnie was such a good person. Arnie really cared about everyone."

"I know, Dovi. I know. Come on, you have to get up. Let's get going now. You want me to help you get dressed?"

"No, I can do it. Go and wait in the living room. Ask Eidel to make you some coffee."

CHAPTER TWENTY-TWO

Dovid was shocked when Fred Lichtenstein sat down at the bar. He'd seen him at the funeral, but Dovid had been too grief-stricken to speak to anyone.

"Levi, how are you holding up?" Fred asked.

Dovid shrugged his shoulders. "I'm here," he sighed.

"I guess you miss Arnie pretty badly."

Dovid swallowed hard and nodded. "More than I can say. So what can I get you, Fred?"

"A beer."

"What kind?"

"Old Style."

Dovid popped the top off of the bottle and put in front of Fred. "You want a glass, or the bottle okay for you?"

"Bottle's fine."

"So what brings you here? I'm sure it's not just to have a drink. Did Arnie owe people money? Because you don't have to worry. I'll make good on his debts. It just might take me some time."

"Owe money?" Fred laughed. "No, boychick. He didn't owe anything. In fact, you're a very rich man. Arnie had almost a million dollars worth of assets. Between his house, which was totally paid off, and the cash he had in the bank, there was more than enough money. And he left it all to you. You're rich, boychick!"

Dovid looked into Fred's eyes.

"I wasn't expecting this," he said. "I'd gladly give it all back to have Arnie here with me again."

"Funny, you know what? He told me that was what you would say. And, by the way, here is a letter that Arnie gave me to give to you when he passed away." Fred took a sealed envelope out of the breast pocket of his suit jacket and handed it to Dovid.

"Did you read it?" Dovid asked Fred.

"No, he told me not to."

"I think I'd like to read this alone," Dovid said.

"I understand," Fred said. "Let's make a date next week when we can get together and I'll show you a list of everything that you've inherited."

Dovid nodded. "Yeah, okay," he said to Fred, holding the letter in his hand. He called out to Harry, who was sitting on a stool outside the snack bar, "Harry, watch the bar for me. I have to go in the back for a few minutes."

Walking into the backroom for the first time since he'd found Arnie gave Dovid a jolt. This was the room where Arnie interviewed him the first time he came in for the job. If he tried, Dovid could imagine Arnie sitting at the small desk in the corner where Arnie paid the bills. He could hear Arnie's laughter and see his eyes. The memories of Arnie giving him fatherly advice were painful because he knew that he would never again be able to call Arnie and ask him what he thought Dovid should do. Dovid stood there, just holding the letter from Arnie in his trembling hand. Then he sunk down into Arnie's chair and felt a terrible sense of loss as he tore open the envelope.

Dovi,

If you're reading this, that means that I must have come to the end of the line. Well, boychick...we all have to go sometime, right? I know you feel like shit right now. But, come on, give me a smile. I shouldn't ask that of you because I know you. And I know you're taking this hard. But listen to me. You were the best friend I ever had. Hell, I called you my son, and let me tell you … I am glad to have had the opportunity to know you. So, don't be sad, Dovi. Open your eyes; you're still young. You have a wonderful future ahead of you. Which brings me to my favorite part of dying … the good part. I am about to give you some wonderful news. You have just inherited the tavern, the car, my house, and a nice load of money that I had lying around. I am sure right now you're thinking, "Arnie, what am I going to do with all of this?" Well, I'm going to tell you what I think you ought to do. Keep the bar open. Don't sell it, because you love it. You love everything about it. I know you have always wanted to make Cool Breeze a manager and give him a raise. Do it. Do it with my blessing.. Give him the chance you always wanted to give him. Maybe you're right. Maybe if Cool Breeze had a job that gave him pride in himself it would help him to fight the addictions that hold him back from being the man you and I both know he could be. Then, if I were you, I would open a second bar. If Cool Breeze is manager of this one, you will have time to build a second. Why not? Be ambitious. Have fun with the money. But most important, boychick, go out and buy that house you have been talking about buying since I met you. You know, the one in the suburbs. The last time you

100

went to look for a home you mentioned a suburb north of the city called Skokie where a lot of Jewish immigrants were moving. Buy a house there if you and your wife like it. Money isn't a problem in your life anymore, so I think you should give Mark a couple of brothers and sisters and a big backyard with a swing set. Then, when he's old enough, tell him the yard is a gift from his Uncle Arnie.

Well, that's all I gotta say for now. I loved you, boychick. I really did. Live a long happy and healthy life and if there really is anything after death, I'll be there waiting for you when you get here.

Love, your friend and Papa,

Arnie.

Dovid felt his eyes sting as the tears ran down his face and dripped onto the paper.

CHAPTER TWENTY-THREE

That Sunday, Dovid and Eidel drove forty-five minutes north of the city to a little village called Skokie. There was open prairie filled with wildflowers and plenty of vacant land but there was also a lot of building going on. They found a lot on a street where several homes were already standing that was only four blocks from a small red brick elementary school.

"How much is the house?" Dovid asked at the model center.

"The three bedroom, two bath with a full finished basement is seventeen thousand dollars," said the woman who worked for the builder.

Seventeen thousand dollars?

Dovid's hands were shaking.

That's a lot of money. But I have it. I can do this. I'm scared, but I'm excited. The only thing that could possibly make this wonderful day even better would be if Arnie were here with me.

Dovid took out his checkbook and wrote a check to the builder for a down payment that day.

When Dovid went into work on Monday, he called Harry into the back room of the bar.

"Listen, Eidel and I bought a house in Skokie yesterday."

"Mazel tov," Harry said, smiling and shaking Dovid's hand.

"Thanks. Listen. I know you and Ida were talking about moving out to the suburbs. How about if I give you some money for a down payment? You can buy your home on the same street as Eidel and me. Our wives are so close; they are like sisters. They would love it. What do you think?"

"I'd love to. But I won't take the money from you as a gift. However, I will take it as a loan. I want to pay you back, Dovi."

"Fair enough. Pay me when you can. So let's take a drive out to Skokie this weekend. Eidel and me, you and Ida. You two can pick out what you want to buy."

"Sounds good. We'll go on Sunday?"

"Yeah," Dovid said. "Sunday. And when you get back to the snack bar, can you make me a hot dog, just mustard? I'm starving."

"Sure thing, Dovi."

Harry got up to leave.

"Harry, also, could you send Cool Breeze back here?"

"Sure."

Cool Breeze came into the back room.

"I heard Mr. Arnie done left you the tavern. It's real sad about him and all. I sure gonna miss him. But I have to say that I sure is glad that you is going to be my boss, Mr. Dovi. I couldn't think of anybody else who I would want to work for more than you."

"Thanks. I appreciate it," Dovid said. "But there is something else, Cool Breeze. There's something I want to ask you. Why don't you sit down?"

"You got somethin' you gotta ask me?" Cool Breeze said, sitting down. "Well ... go on, ask, Mister Dovi."

"How would you like to be the manager of this place?"

"What? Me?" Cool Breeze looked genuinely shocked.

"Yes, you. I will give you a nice raise. I won't be around here all the time, so you'll be in charge of everything, including keeping the customers in line.

"What about Mr. Harry?"

"I am going to give him the snack bar. That will be his business. He will own it. You will be in charge of the tavern, the entertainment, the ordering, the bills. You can do it, Cool Breeze. I know you can."

"Where you gonna be?"

"I'm looking at opening a second location across the street from Garfield Park."

"No kiddin!'" Cool Breeze laughed. "You sure is somethin' else, Mister Dovi."

CHAPTER TWENTY-FOUR

On August 28, 1963, Dr. Martin Luther King gave a speech that spoke of a world in which hate and prejudice no longer existed; a world where the color of a man's skin did not define him. Dovi, Harry, and Cool Breeze watched it on television at the bar. Dovi caught Cool Breeze's eyes.

"This speech that we are watching is the beginning of something earth-shattering. There is going to be real change all around us. Change for the better. My whole body is tingling. It's all unfolding right before our eyes. I don't know about the two of you, but it takes my breath away. A wonderful thing like this could only happen in a country like America. Watch and see. This Dr. King, along with the help of President Kennedy, will change the way that black men are treated," Dovid said.

"You called us blacks and not colored," Cool Breeze smiled.

"You call me Jewish and not kike. You should know that I have always wanted to be respectful of you and your people. I only ever used the term 'colored' because that was the only term I'd ever heard. But you know me, Cool Breeze. You know I've never been influenced by the color of a man's skin. Just the way you've never said anything bad about Harry and me being Jews. You, me, and Harry are like the Three Musketeers in Dumas' book. We're the best of friends. Isn't that right, Harry?"

"Absolutely," Harry said.

The speech was called the "I have a dream speech," and what a magnificent dream it is...

CHAPTER TWENTY-FIVE

By the time the Levis' new house was finished in late September of 1963, Eidel was four months pregnant with their second child. She was due to deliver in January. Because of this, Dovid hired movers to do everything. He insisted that Eidel not lift a finger.

At the end of November, Eidel moved into her new home. Everything had been neatly put away on shelves and in drawers for her.

Three weeks later, Ida and Harry moved into their house. They chose a smaller model because they knew they would not have children and so they didn't need the extra space.

Dovid insisted that he and Eidel join the newly formed synagogue on Dempster Street, right in the heart of Skokie. It was a brand new building. Rabbi Mittleman welcomed Dovid Levi and his wife with open arms.

I may not be religious, but joining the temple will be good for my family. It will give us a sense of community. I want my children to grow up proud of being Jewish, Dovid thought as he made a generous donation to the shul.

The Levis' new home had a full finished basement that had a bathroom, complete with a shower and tub. Having all this extra room in the house, Dovid could see no reason for Cool Breeze to continue renting rooms in a flophouse. He talked to Eidel and convinced her to allow Cool Breeze to move in with them and live in the basement.

"He's really handy. He'll be a big help if we need to fix anything around here."

"I've heard you and Harry talking … he drinks? He shoots drugs? Do you think it's safe for him to be around our children?"

"Absolutely. I trust him completely. He has addiction problems but he would never hurt us," Dovid said. "He has been going to some kind of a program for addicts. He's been doing really well. And he does a great job managing the bar. What more could we ask for?"

"All right, let him move in," Eidel said, shrugging her shoulders.

And so Cool Breeze moved into the Levis' basement.

Every afternoon, Harry, Cool Breeze, and Dovid rode to work together.

CHAPTER TWENTY-SIX

November 1963

Dovid was stocking the bar, Cool Breeze was sweeping the floor, and Harry was cleaning out the ice bins. The radio was playing in the background. Dovid had a pencil and paper in front of him. He was adding up the cost of tile for the floor of the new bar when the music on the radio stopped. An announcer in a solemn voice said, "Ladies and Gentlemen, we interrupt this program to tell you that President John Fitzgerald Kennedy has been shot."

Dovid didn't hear the announcement. He wasn't paying attention. He was too busy calculating. Cool Breeze called out to Harry and Dovid. "Did you hear what that man on the radio said? Kennedy done been shot."

"Isn't he in Texas today?" Harry said.

"Ain't sure," Cool Breeze said.

"One of you turn on the TV. You're both standing right over there. Turn it on. Let's see what the hell is going on," Dovid said.

By nightfall it was all over the news; President Kennedy was dead. He was shot in the head in Dallas Texas. This was the death of not only a president but also a loss of innocence. Before that day in 1964, no one believed that the assassination of the president would happen in a country like America in the 1960s. For years to come, people would discuss the death of JFK and remember exactly where they were when they learned the dreadful news.

December brought a terrible winter storm. The heavy snowfall stopped all construction on the bar that Dovid was having built across from Garfield Park. The city was paralyzed by the mountains of snow and by the icy winds that came rushing off Lake Michigan. On the first two days of the storm it was impossible to drive so all three men missed work. By the third day, the salt trucks came through the city, melting the snow enough for Dovid to navigate the roads and to get to the bar with Cool Breeze and Harry and open it.

Surprisingly, even in the bad weather, the bar was busy. People in the neighborhood did not have to go into work or school, and so they walked over to the tavern where they met up with their friends, had a beer, a whiskey, or a burger and passed the cold winter days.

By the end of the week, the city had returned to normal. Schools reopened and the roads were fairly clear.

However, the weather had halted the construction of Dovid's second tavern. Now the builders had moved the date of completion to the spring of 1964.

CHAPTER TWENTY-SEVEN

Chicago, 1964

On the thirteenth of January at four-thirty in the morning, Eidel gave birth to a healthy baby girl. She entered the world with a lusty cry and a full head of dark curly hair. When the nurse placed the infant in Eidel's arms, something strange happened to Eidel. She suddenly had a brief flashback to the day so long ago when she was just a child and Zofia Weiss had come to her home. Eidel looked into the face of her daughter and chills ran through her.

My baby looks like my birth mother.

Eidel couldn't understand why looking at this child frightened her. It shouldn't have. The little girl was beautiful. Her tiny features were perfect. And yet, the baby's resemblance to her birth mother scared Eidel.

Dovid looked down into the blanket at his new daughter. "She's so pretty, isn't she?" he said.

"Yes, that she is …" Eidel was overcome with a mixture of strange emotions. She began to cry.

"What is it? What's wrong, my love? Can I get you anything?"

Eidel shook her head. "I'm sorry, Dovid. I think I just need to be alone. Can you please ask the nurse to come and take the baby back to the nursery?"

"Of course. Do you feel all right?" Dovid was worried. Eidel looked pale, as if something had upset her. When Dovid was younger and worked with his father he'd seen women die of infection. He put his hand on Eidel's head to see if her body temperature was raised but her forehead felt cool. "I'll have the nurse take her for a while and then I'll stay here with you."

"No, Dovid. I'd rather be alone," Eidel said. "Is Ida here?"

"She's on her way."

"Tell the nurses to let her in."

"Eidel, what is it?"

She shook her head. "I just want to be alone for a while," she snapped.

Later, when Ida got to the hospital, Eidel tried to explain her feelings to her best friend.

"I just feel so sad. But I also feel scared, in a way. I don't know why. I didn't feel any of this when Mark was born." She hesitated; then continued. "Do you remember the story I told you about my birth mother?"

"Of course," Ida said, sitting at Eidel's bedside, holding her hand. "How could I forget such a thing?"

"This baby makes me uncomfortable. I don't remember exactly what Zofia Weiss looked like, but from what I can remember, the baby looks just like her. It makes me question who I am, who my birth mother was. I don't know … I don't know."

Ida squeezed Eidel's hand.

"You are Eidel Levi and this precious little girl is your daughter."

"I know, and I feel terrible because I don't want to hold her. I don't want to nurse her. I don't even want to look at her. I just don't know what's come over me."

"You have to be a mother to this infant. Pull yourself together, Eidel. Whatever is upsetting you is not the baby's fault. The child can't help that she reminds you of someone and it makes you uneasy. This little girl lying in the nursery right now is your child, Eidel, and she needs you."

Eidel shook her head.

"I understand and I realize this. But my milk isn't coming in. Not like it did with Mark. I am going to have to put her on formula. Can you feed her when the nurses bring her? Can you do that for me Ida? The truth is, please don't tell Dovid, but I can't bear to hold her."

Ida nodded. She was genuinely worried about Eidel. "Yes, of course. You're my best friend, Eidel. I would do anything for you."

Dovid asked Eidel if she wanted to name the baby for Helen. It was, after all, her turn to name one of their children for her mother. He'd named their first child for his father. Eidel refused. Instead, she said that because Arnie had been so good to them she wanted to name the baby for Arnie, with a middle name for Dovid's mother. Dovid didn't argue. He was thrilled to be able to give Arnie a namesake. He suggested Abby Ruth Levi. Eidel shrugged and agreed.

Abby wasn't an easy baby the way that Mark had been. She had colic, cried constantly, and hardly slept. Nothing seemed to soothe little Abby. It was as if she knew her mother didn't like her. Even as an infant, she seemed to have a chip on her shoulder. Her digestive system resisted the formula and so everything she ate came right back up, leaving her constantly hungry, and demanding that her parents find a solution.

Dovid was busy with work. He was juggling the existing bar while trying to build the new one. Although he knew Eidel was having problems with Abby, he didn't want to see the problems. Eidel was just not bonding with their daughter. Abby was a red-faced, fussy infant who pushed off with her hands and feet if Eidel even tried to cuddle her. Ida would arrive at the Levi home to find Eidel in tears and the baby screaming in her crib. Since Abby's birth, Eidel had lost a lot of weight. She was skinny and gaunt. This baby was a fighter and was far more than she could handle. Ida could see that her friend was sleep deprived and so she insisted that Eidel rest while she tried to take care of Abby. Eidel would lie down, but she could hear Abby's continuous wailing from her room. She heard the heels of Ida's shoes as they met the hardwood floor, and Eidel knew that Ida was pacing the floor with Abby in her arms trying to quiet the child.

Ida even signed up and took driving lessons from a driving school. She siphoned the money to pay for the lessons out of her grocery money each week. Once her instructor said she was ready, Ida took the test and got her license. Now she would have to convince Harry to buy her a used car.

"I've heard that the motion of a car puts a baby to sleep," Ida told Eidel.

"You think Harry will get you a car?" Eidel asked.

"I don't know. I hope so. All I can tell you is, I'll try."

After several days of giving Harry a convincing argument

why she needed an automobile, he finally agreed to buy Ida an older-model used car.

"I don't even have a car. But my wife, she needs a car," Harry said, throwing his hands up in the air. "I can never win an argument with you, my darling."

"I love you, Harry. This will make my trips to buy groceries so much easier. And I will be able to take Eidel with the children to pick up meat and bread as well. You know how hard it is to get to the stores, especially in winter. Most of the time we have to wait for Dovid to take all of us on Sunday and he is always so tired. He hates to drive everyone to the stores and wait while we shop. My having a car will be good for everyone. And as soon as you have a little bit of spare time, you should go and get your license. You can use the car too. It would be good for you to be able to get around without buses or bothering Dovi."

Harry just smiled. When Ida wanted something from him, if it was in his power, she got it. They took a bus together to a used car lot where Harry purchased an inexpensive automobile. "Now don't be going all over the place. Gas costs money. Besides, I don't want you to get lost," Harry said to Ida, handing her the keys.

She smiled. Then she leaned over and kissed him.

The automobile didn't work to soothe Abby at all. She just screamed while Ida was driving. It didn't even help with Eidel's depression. But the ability to drive did give Ida a new-found freedom. She began taking classes for adults at the library. She took language classes in English and also lessons in cooking and baking. Since the classes were only a couple of hours, three times a week, she still had plenty of time to help Eidel with the children.

One evening, Mark was napping and with lots of coaxing Abby had finally fallen asleep. Ida was about to leave. She would go home and prepare some food so it was ready when Harry got home in the morning. Then she'd take a hot bath and lay down. Abby was a big job and as much as Ida loved her, that angry little infant was draining Ida too.

"Ida, stay for a few minutes and have a cup of tea with me, please," Eidel implored.

Harry wouldn't be home until four in the morning. Ida would have liked to leave but she saw the distress in Eidel's face. Ida sat down at the kitchen table. Eidel put a pot of water on the stove to boil.

"I am ashamed to admit this, but I don't like my daughter. I think I hate Abby."

"You don't hate her. Don't even say that."

"She is making my life miserable. Mark wasn't like this. I know that it is hard work to take care of a baby. I realize that but this one … is impossible. God forgive me, but I can't stand her."

"Oh, Eidel. You can't mean it. A child is such a blessing."

"This child, Ida? This child? Tell me you honestly believe that?"

"Yes, all children. Abby will grow out of this stage. You'll see. And then she will be a wonderful loving daughter. Give her a chance, Eidel."

"She hates me. I try to hold her and she turns away from me. She is crying and fighting so hard because even though she is an infant she already knows that she doesn't want to be my child. And you know what? Dovid doesn't even notice.

He doesn't even care. He just goes about his life. My life has been ruined since Abby was born. But he is doing just fine. He has no idea." Tears were running down Eidel's cheeks. "Sometimes, I want to die," she said.

That was when Ida knew she had to intervene and talk to Dovid. Something was terribly wrong with Eidel and it was not going to go away without help.

CHAPTER TWENTY-EIGHT

Two days passed since Ida and Eidel talked about Abby. It was late afternoon, just a half hour before the tavern was scheduled to open. Dovid was sitting at the bar, meeting with the builders for the new nightclub. The local blues band that was playing at the bar that night had just come in to set up their equipment. Dovid took a pile of papers from one of the builders and shook his hand. The builder smiled and left. Dovid went behind the bar and poured himself a draft beer then sat down at the counter and began to look through the paperwork. Harry was setting up the snack bar on the other side of the room, while Cool Breeze was stocking the shelves with whiskey.

"I'm excited about this new business. I think it's going to be a real adventure. This is different than anything we've done so far. This new place is going to be an upscale nightclub in a ritzy area," Dovid said, taking a long sip of the golden brew.

"Well, at least you probably ain't gonna have no fights there," Cool Breeze said when Dovid told him about the plans. "This is gonna be a whole new experience for you, Mister Dovi."

"Yes, it will. How do you like managing the tavern?"

"I like it. I like it a lot."

"Good. I just wanted to let you know that you're doing a really good job."

"Thank you, Mister Dovi. You know, I don't know if I ever told you, but I really do appreciate the opportunities that you done gave me. You been a good friend all these years."

"We are like family, all of us. You, me, Harry, Arnie, he should rest in peace. Arnie …"

"We sure enough is."

"You know, you don't have to call me Mister Dovi; you can just call me Dovi."

"Yeah, but I ain't gonna do that. I been callin' you Mister Dovi for too long to start callin' you just by your name."

"It's up to you. But I call you, Cool Breeze. You can call me Dovi."

Just then Ida walked into the bar. Harry rushed from behind the snack bar over to her side. They spoke to each other for several minutes in whispers. Harry nodded as if she'd told him something and he understood. Dovid sat very still, watching them. He was waiting to see how he might help.

Ida wouldn't come to the bar unless there was something wrong. I can't believe Ida drove all the way down here from Skokie. She wouldn't be coming for no good reason. Something is happening. God, I hope it's not Eidel or the baby.

Ida had been going to the Levi house to help Eidel with Abby every day since the child was born. Since Ida had gone back to school, she worked her visits with Eidel into her class schedule but she was there every day for at least a few hours to give Eidel a break.

Ida left Harry's side and began to walk towards Dovid. Dovid felt his heart pounding in his chest.

Oh God, what is it that's wrong?

"Dovi, I need to talk to you."

"Is everything all right?"

"Yes and no. Everybody is fine. I mean, physically everybody is fine. But, Dovid, Eidel is not right since the birth of Abby. She is very depressed. She won't eat and she refuses to hold the new baby. Now I know Abby can be difficult, but Eidel is Abby's mother. The child needs her. Eidel has gotten so bad that lately she even pushes Mark away from her when he cries. Now don't get me wrong, I don't mind helping with the children. But you should know this is happening. I am worried about her, Dovid."

Dovid bit his lower lip.

"How did you get here? Did you drive all this way?" he asked.

"No, I took the L. I was afraid to drive on the highway. I thought I might get lost."

"You took the L here? Do you want something to eat or drink?"

"No, Dovid, I need to talk to you, that's why I came."

"Here, come, sit down at the bar and we can talk."

"I need to talk to you alone," Ida said. "I know it's a lot to ask, but can you leave for an hour or so to take me back home? We can talk more about this on the way."

"Yes, sure, of course." Dovie was clearly shaken by what Ida had just told him. And he realized that even though Ida and Eidel were best friends, the Levis were asking a lot of Ida.

"I'll be right back. I have to get the car keys."

Dovid grabbed his car keys off the desk in the back room. He told Harry and Cool Breeze he was going to drive Ida home and he'd be back in about forty-SIX minutes.

They rode in silence for a while. Dovid was traumatized. Eidel had to be in bad shape for Ida to have taken the L all the way to the South Side to speak to him. He had not been expecting this, and he'd never been alone in an automobile with his best friend's wife. Although he had no unsavory intentions, he still felt awkward and uncomfortable. Still, he knew that Ida was very close to Eidel and she knew everything that was going on in his home. He realized that he hadn't wanted to know, but now he had to ask her to tell him. This was the only way he could help his wife.

"We are alone now. You can tell me what's going on with Eidel."

"I am worried sick about her. She has been sinking into a depression for a while. But since the birth of the baby, she is inconsolable. Sometimes she cries for hours. I cannot tempt her to eat, no matter what I prepare for her. This may sound crazy, but I am afraid that she might take her own life. That is why I came to see you. As you know, Eidel is my best friend here in America. We are like sisters."

"I know that you are close to her and I believe you that she isn't doing well. I have seen bits and pieces of it, but I have just been so busy with my work that I haven't paid attention. I guess I was hoping it would go away..." Dovid said, ashamed of himself. "What do you think I should do? How can I help her?"

"I don't know. Maybe she needs to see a doctor," Ida said. "She might be ill."

"Is it all right if I tell her that you spoke to me?" he asked.

"She knows already. I told her I was going to go to the bar to see you. Eidel and I have no secrets between us. Like I said, she is my best friend. I will do whatever you need me to do in order to help her."

"You have been caring for the children since Abby was born. I've noticed that Eidel has never liked Abby. I thought that she would come out of it, but she hasn't."

"Yes, that's right. I want you to know that I will continue to help Eidel with the children until she gets better. Then, if it's all right with you, maybe you can find someone to come in and help her."

"Yes, of course," Dovid said. "I'm going to drop you off at your house. I'm going to stay home with Eidel for the rest of the night. I'll call the bar and tell Harry and Cool Breeze to take a taxi back when the bar closes. I want to get in touch with a doctor right away."

"I think it's a good idea," Ida said.

CHAPTER TWENTY-NINE

Although it was early evening, Eidel was already in bed when Dovid got home. Both children were asleep in their rooms.

Dovid tiptoed into the bedroom he shared with his wife.

"Hello, my love," he said, leaning down and kissing Eidel's cheek.

She opened her eyes and stared at him. "What are you doing home so early?"

"You know that Ida came to see me today?"

"Yes, I know, she told me she was going to the bar. I told her she was crazy to take the L. I told her she could talk to you on Sunday. I'm fine, Dovid."

"Are you, Eidel?"

"I don't know. I guess I am," she said. He sat down on the edge of the bed.

"I'm concerned about you. Do you feel all right?"

"Sometimes, sometimes not."

"What is it Eidel? What is bothering you?"

There was a long silence. The room was dark. Dovid heard his wife sigh.

"I don't think I love you anymore, Dovid. I'm sorry," she said, her voice barely a whisper. "I don't want to be a mother or a wife. I think I want to go home to Poland. I think I want to convert to Catholicism and become a nun."

Dovid felt his brow crease. "You want a divorce? That's unheard of. What have I done?"

"I don't care what's unheard of Dovid. I am miserable here," she said. "I want to leave you and these children and go back home."

Dovid crossed his arms over his chest. He was unable to speak for a few minutes. "Eidel. If you want a divorce, I'll give you one. But will you do something for me first?"

"What?"

"Will you agree to see a doctor? I will take you in the morning if you will go with me. Let's just see if maybe he can help you to feel better."

"I don't know. I don't really want to go to a doctor."

"Please, Eidel. Please, do this one thing for me."

"All right. I'll go with you. But if it doesn't help, I want to go home. And I want a divorce. Fair enough?"

"Yes," he nodded.

CHAPTER THIRTY

Dovid took care of the children when they woke up from their nap. Because Eidel had put them down so late, it was impossible to get them to go to bed at a reasonable hour. Dovid fed them and bathed them. He played with them until they finally went to sleep at eleven that night. Eidel never came out of her room.

How long has she been like this? Have I been so wrapped up in my business that I never noticed? Am I too late to save this marriage?

The following morning after Ida arrived to watch the children, Dovid and Eidel left the house. They were on their way to see Dr. Silverman. Arnie had recommended him and he had delivered both of their children. He knew the Levis, especially Eidel, fairly well.

The doctor's waiting room was filled with women, most of them pregnant. Dovid was the only man there. He didn't care. All he wanted was to do whatever was necessary to bring his wife back to him.

"Mrs. Levi," the nurse called.

"That's us," Dovid said, smiling at Eidel. She didn't return his smile. She just nodded.

They were escorted into a room where the nurse gave Eidel a gown to change into. "Would you like your husband to wait outside while you change?"

Eidel gave a short laugh. "No. That's not necessary."

Dr. Silverman came in a few minutes later carrying a file in his hand.

"Eidel, how are you feeling?"

She shrugged.

"Doctor, my wife has been very depressed lately. She isn't eating. She has no interest in the children. Most of the day, she lays in a dark room."

"Who is caring for your babies right now, Eidel?"

"A friend," Eidel said, turning her attention out the window.

"Who takes care of them most of the time?"

"The same friend."

"Eidel, don't you want to raise your children?" the doctor asked gently.

Eidel shrugged, still not looking directly at the doctor.

"Mr. Levi," Dr. Silverman turned to Dovid and asked, "Can I speak with your wife alone for a few minutes?"

"Sure, yes, of course," Dovid stammered. "I'll be in the waiting room."

"That would be perfect. When Eidel and I have finished speaking, I will have the nurse come out and get you."

Dovid shook his head and left the room. He paced the waiting room in spite of the fact that he knew he was probably making the other patients nervous. But he couldn't sit still. Finally, after fifteen minutes, the nurse opened the door and called his name.

"Mr. Levi. The doctor would like you to come in now."

Dovid's hands were trembling as he was escorted into an office instead of an examining room. Eidel was not there.

"Mr. Levi. I wanted to speak with you alone. Please, won't you sit down?" Dr. Silverman said.

"Where is Eidel?" Dovid asked.

"She's getting dressed. Don't worry about her. One of my nurses is with her. I need to talk to you."

"Go ahead, talk, please." Dovid felt his hands trembling.

"Your wife has a condition known as post-partum depression. It's a nervous condition. She needs professional help. I am recommending that you send her to a hospital that is on the northwest side of the city. They handle this sort of thing and I think they will be able to help her."

"What kind of hospital?"

"A mental hospital."

"Dunning? You're talking about sending my Eidel to Dunning?"

"That's a rather informal name for the place, but yes. I think she needs help and they can give her what she needs."

"Dunning is a state hospital for the insane. It has a terrible reputation. People talk about it like it is a trip right to hell. I don't know if I can do that to Eidel. I just don't know. I have money, I can pay for a private hospital."

"They will do the same things to help her at a private hospital as they would at a state hospital. My guess is she will probably need some sort of shock therapy."

Dovid felt a wave of nausea. He had been getting migraines lately. They always began with him seeing small black dots in his eyes. His head ached, and he was seeing the spots.

"Let me think about this," Dovid said, clearing his throat. Then he went on. "I can't just commit her. I need to take some time to give this some thought. I am sorry, but I have to be sure. Give me the night to go over this in my mind. I'll call you in the morning."

"Very well. I realize that this is a difficult decision. But I think it's the right one. However, if you prefer a private hospital, I understand, and I think I can help you find a good fit."

"Like I said, I'll call you tomorrow."

"I understand. I'll be waiting for your call. For now, go out into the waiting room. I'll send Eidel there to meet you."

CHAPTER THIRTY-ONE

Dovid and Eidel did not speak on the way home. When they arrived, she went into her bedroom and he left the house. There was a small neighborhood diner on Touhy and Crawford, about four blocks from the Levis' home. Dovid decided to walk there. It was early December and it was cold, but he needed the fresh air to think.

At first, his mind was whirling too fast for him to sort out his thoughts. He walked and watched his breath as it came out white in the freezing air.

Where did our lives together go wrong? I have been working hard. I know I have been gone a lot, but it is only so that I could provide a good life for my family. I wanted to be a good husband and father but somehow I've lost everything.

I can remember how beautiful things were between Eidel and me. When we made love it was like two puzzle pieces fitting together. Her smile could brighten my whole day. Her laughter soothed my soul and made me believe that I could conquer the world. I've given her material things, but obviously, I've failed her. I've failed her miserably. And lately I am always so tired that our lovemaking has become a quick fifteen-minute affair a few times a month.

We hardly go out, because I work every night. And when I get home during the day, I sleep. She has Ida, and I know that they are the best of friends. But Ida is not her husband. Eidel must be feeling unloved and alone.

Dovid got to the restaurant and ordered a cup of coffee. He

sat in a booth alone in the back, sipping the steamy liquid.

I refuse to put my beloved bershart into a crazy house. I won't do it. I won't let them scramble her brain because I was too busy to give her the love she needed.

What the hell is the matter with me? I don't need this second bar. I don't even need to work. Cool Breeze is a great manager. Harry's business is thriving. I can spend time with Eidel. We can travel, make love, start our marriage over. This is what I must do. I am going to go home and stop the plans for the new building for the bar across from Garfield. Then I am going to talk to Harry and Cool Breeze. Eidel and I will become like young lovers again. No matter what it takes I will never give up on my wife.

Ida was at the Levis' house with the children. She was giving Abby a bottle when Dovid knocked softly on the door.

"Come in," she said.

He entered then he asked her if she would be willing to care for the children for four days while he and Eidel spent a little time at a hotel downtown. Ida readily agreed. Dovid offered to pay her, but she adamantly refused. She'd grown to love Mark and Abby. Ida was like a second mother to them.

Next, Dovid booked a room at the Blackstone, a posh hotel on Michigan Avenue. Then he went into the bedroom and turned on the light. Eidel rubbed her eyes. Dovid realized he'd probably awakened her.

"Pack your bags, we're going downtown."

"For what?"

"For a vacation. For a second honeymoon. I thought you might like to walk with me, hand in hand, down State Street and look at the Christmas lights in the window of Marshall

130

Field's."

"You don't like to celebrate Christmas."

"But I love you. And I know this is something you would enjoy doing. So it would make me happy to do it with you. If you want to, we can even look at the decorations on the big Catholic church that's downtown. I am sure it is decorated beautifully for the holiday."

"Really? You would do that for me?"

"Eidel. I would do anything for you. Don't you think I realize how hard this has been for you? You were raised to be a Catholic and then, all of a sudden, out of nowhere you find out your birth mother was Jewish. It's confusing. And I know that it has been difficult for you to learn English. Especially with me working all the time. Thank God for Ida."

"Yes, Ida has been a godsend. She is my angel." Eidel smiled. "You're surprising me, Dovi. I never thought you paid much attention to how I feel."

"Oh, my love, you are so wrong. I pay attention to everything. Yes, I have been busy working, building our future. But all of it has been for you and for our children. I don't want to lose you. Give me the chance and I promise you I will bring the man you fell in love with back to you. And, with God's help, you will fall for me again."

CHAPTER THIRTY-TWO

The Blackstone Hotel, with its marble floors, crystal chandeliers, and plush guestrooms was the perfect backdrop for romance. Dovid and Eidel took a taxi to State Street to look at the decorations in the window of Marshall Field's. A light snow brushed the ground as they watched the tiny electric train follow it's track through the little Christmas village in the store window. They went inside the store and upstairs to its restaurant where they had hot cocoa and pastries for breakfast. Then they walked hand in hand as they passed the line of children waiting to sit on Santa's lap.

Dovid made reservations for dinner that night at the Blackhawk restaurant.

"I don't have a dress that is fancy enough for such a place," Eidel said.

"Well, then, let's go shopping," Dovid winked at her. "I can't wait to see my beautiful wife try on all the latest styles."

They spent the rest of the day going to all of the big department stores downtown. By the time four o'clock rolled around, Eidel was laughing and having fun trying on all of the lovely clothes for Dovid who waited outside each dressing room.

Finally, they both decided on a black cashmere fitted dress with silk stockings and matching leather pumps.

They arrived at the Blackhawk at eight and were seated at a

candlelit table with a white tablecloth. Dovid ordered prime rib and stuffed baked potatoes for two.

That night when they returned to their room Dovid suggested that Eidel take a hot shower. "It's so cold outside, it will help you to shake the chill," he said.

After the water was running for a few minutes, Dovid did something bold that he'd never done before. He removed his clothes and got in the shower with Eidel. At first when he saw the shock on her face, he thought about apologizing and leaving the bathroom. But then she laughed. Once he heard that sweet laughter, he knew he was on the right track. He just needed to show Eidel how much he still loved her and soon enough he would break down that wall of depression that Eidel had buried herself under. Dovid kissed his wife slowly but passionately. Then he took her in his arms and pulled her close to him. She sighed.

"It's been a long time since I felt this way when we touched, Dovi."

"I know. It's been too long. I am never going to neglect you again. We have plenty of money now. I'll go in to check on things at the bar twice a week, but most of my time will be spent with you. We can travel, maybe go to California or Canada in the spring. Whatever you want."

"We can decide in the spring. Right now, kiss me Dovi, kiss me and keep kissing me all through the night."

CHAPTER THIRTY-THREE

1965

Dovid had never celebrated Valentine's Day. It was, of course, not a Jewish holiday. But since it was a special day for lovers in America, he was planning surprises that he knew Eidel would enjoy. He asked Ida to take the children. While Eidel took the children to drop them off at Ida's home, he had a fancy dinner catered by a local restaurant delivered to the Levi house. He filled the bedroom he shared with Eidel with rose petals. When Eidel returned from Ida's house, the table was set for two with candles and wine glasses. Dovid took Eidel's hand and led her to her chair. Then they ate a decadent dinner, after which Dovid presented Eidel a box of expensive chocolates. He opened the box and took a round piece of dark chocolate and fed her a bite, then he tasted the candy himself.

"You've changed so much Dovi," Eidel said.

"I don't want to lose you. I got caught up in other things and I forgot how important it was for me to show you how much you mean to me."

"I have never been as happy as I've been since we have been working on our marriage."

"I'm glad, my love. This is what I have been hoping for."

They made love through the night. Dovid could see Eidel

reverting back to the girl he'd married. She was laughing more, but she still had moments when he would catch her looking out the window with tears threatening to spill out of her eyes. Dovid had never shied away from a challenge and he wasn't about to give up on his wife.

Ida had not only been a good friend, but she'd saved their marriage by helping with the children during Eidel's emotional recovery. So, for her birthday, Dovid and Eidel gave Ida and Harry a trip to Florida for a week. Dovid agreed to go in every day and work Harry's restaurant inside the tavern. Eidel said she understood and she agreed that it was a good idea for Harry and Ida to get away for a while. Dovid and Eidel had been spending all of their time together.

"It's only a week. But are you sure you'll be all right without me at home or Ida around?"

"I will, Dovi," Eidel said, taking his hand. "I'm glad we can do this for Harry and Ida."

"But can you handle the children on your own?" He was worried that she was still unstable. But she smiled and nodded and something in her smile reassured him that she was going to be fine. The Rosens left on a Sunday morning. Dovid and Eidel took them to the airport. It felt strange to Dovid to be working so many hours again during that week but the separation from his wife made the passion between Dovid and Eidel even greater when Dovid got home. He was tired, but he found that he'd missed his wife. Their time together that week was limited and so it became even more precious. And Dovid, who had once loved to work, found that he was glad when Harry returned from his trip.

Eidel was like a flower and Dovid was like the sun. Every day she opened up a little more to him. They began to really talk to each other, to really communicate. She talked about how much she missed her mother and her past and even admitted that she'd gone and sat in a church one afternoon because it brought back so many memories. Dovid listened to her without judgment. He held her as she wept for her mother. He comforted her when she told him of how insecure she was about fitting into American culture. And she admitted that she couldn't seem to feel close to Abby. This worried Dovid. "I want to love her, Dovi. Maybe as she gets older ..."

Many times Dovid got up with Abby in the middle of the night. He warmed her bottle and gently rocked her back to sleep. Dovid didn't mind. He loved his spirited little girl with the curly black mane and he wanted Eidel to get her rest. He hoped that if Abby was not a burden to Eidel then perhaps she would start to feel warmly towards the child. Dovid felt that things were getting better between Eidel and himself. They made love more these days than they had in the beginning of their marriage. Now it was just a matter of Eidel and Abby growing close like a normal mother and daughter. Dovid had confidence that over time it would happen.

By November, Eidel was pregnant again.

CHAPTER THIRTY-FOUR

Spring 1965

It was early spring. The frigid winter cold was giving way. The freezing temperatures were growing milder. It was still cool, but not nearly as frigid as it had been. The snow of winter was beginning to melt, leaving the ground a mess of brown slush.

Since Dovid had stopped working he was on a more normal schedule. He got up in the morning and slept at night. He and Eidel had breakfast together. Sometimes, Ida came over and spent a few hours but she didn't come as much as she used to. Dovid and Eidel spent most of their days together, either reading, watching TV, or playing cards or checkers. Eidel no longer did the food shopping. Dovid went to the stores in his car while Eidel watched the babies at home. Every Sunday they still had dinner with Ida and Harry. Sometimes they went out, other times one of the women cooked.

Cool Breeze was still living with them. However, because of his hours, Dovid only saw him when he was leaving for work. One afternoon, Cool Breeze came upstairs an hour early to see Dovid before he left for work. Harry had recently gotten a driver's license and drove Cool Breeze and himself to work.

"Mister Dovi, have you been watching the news?"

Dovi shook his head.

"You remember that black fella who was good friends with President Kennedy?"

"Dr. King?"

"Yeah, he the one. He's got a whole big group of colored folks and they is marching for equality."

"I like him. I heard his speech," Dovid said.

"He gonna change the world for the colored man. You wait and see."

"I hope so, Cool Breeze. If I learned anything from living through the war, it's that nothing good comes from prejudice. Hatred destroys not only the victims, but it also destroys the persecutors."

"You mean the folks who do bad things to others because they be black or Jewish?"

"Yes, I do. People who hurt other people cannot ever really be happy, Cool Breeze. Love and compassion is the only route to true happiness."

"Now you sounds like Jesus Christ."

Dovid laughed. "I've never read anything about Jesus. Never read the words he spoke or his philosophy. In fact, the last time I read a religious text was when I was studying for my bar mitzvah. I was thirteen. I have to tell you the truth. I don't follow any religion. My religion is to be good to other people, to be kind. That's all I believe. Treat people right. And… I tell you what. I am not sure, but I think there just might be a God."

"I do think so," Cool Breeze said. "He brung me to Arnie

and then to you. Hell, I was stayin' in a flophouse. Never knew where my next meal was coming from. Drinkin,' shootin' smack, just waitin' for the end. Then one day, I was standing outside trying to beg some change to get me some booze when Arnie drives by in his big ol' cadi. He opens the window and says, 'Hey you, you want to make a few extra bucks? I need help at my bar today.' So, I says sure."

"That's how you met Arnie?"

"Yeah. But that wasn't all. I come to work for him. After I been with him for less than a week he paid money to put me in a hospital where I got clean for a while. Then I be sad to tell you, but I slipped back. Shit … he be so disappointed in me. I be so disappointed in me too. But even though I done that Arnie still didn't fire me."

"He put you in a hospital? I once asked him to do that and he refused. He never told me that he did it in the past."

"He didn't want to tell you cause he knew I was ashamed cause I failed. Fell off the wagon and failed."

"Cool Breeze, are you straight now? Are you off the heroin?" And I aint drinkin' neither."

"Yes, Mister Dovi. I been straight for almost a year. Being around the alcohol at the tavern sure is hard for me. But I loves that job. When I goes to work I feels like I am somebody now. I got a feeling of pride. I be a manager."

"You sure are. I hope that Dr. King can help more colored people to find better jobs. I believe that the Negro race needs a leg up. They need a little help."

"There be so many white folks that don't feel like you does, Mister Dovi. They think the black man ought to still be a slave."

"They're just ignorant, Breeze. There was a time in history that Jews were slaves too. Did you know that?"

"In Egypt, right?"

"Yes, right."

"My mother be a God fearin' woman. She be a good woman. We goed to church every Sunday. She learned my brothers and sisters and me the bible. That's how I knowed that Jews was slaves in them Egyptian times. You see, I weren't raised bad. I just got in with the wrong crowd when I be a teenager. That's how I started drinkin'. Drugs comed later. But it sure weren't my Mama's fault. It's hard to be a colored man comin' up in the south. I was borned in a small town in Mississippi. White folks in the south treat colored folks real bad. My brothers and sisters bowed their heads when they seed a white man. But, not me. I got mean. Then I got in trouble. I got into a fight and hurt a white boy. Spent some years in jail. When I got out, I headed for Chicago where didn't nobody know me. I figured because it was in the north it would be better for a colored man. But, I didn't have no money, got involved with running numbers. Then drugs. Like I said, Mister Arnie helped me a lot."

"I'm glad, Cool Breeze. You're a smart man. You have a lot to offer the world."

"You know I hear that lots of white folks is scared of Dr. King. They be afraid that he gonna cause trouble and try to take over the President's house. They know that colored folks be angry. The folks what done us wrong, know they done us wrong. So they be afraid of Dr. King and they be afraid of us colored gathering in a group. They think we gonna get violent."

"I'm not afraid of the colored or of Dr. King. But I am a little afraid for him. That President Kennedy tried to change things and he was assassinated. I just hope Dr. King is careful and that he has plenty of security. People try to destroy that which they fear, my friend."

"Yes, I do knows that. And, Mister Dovi, you has no reason to be afraid. You always been fair with me and every other colored person I ever seed you talk to. Sometimes I think you don't even see the difference in races."

"I don't, Cool Breeze. I have seen too much death because of differences that are only imaginary. Under our skin, we are all the same, whether we are Christian, Jewish, Colored, White, Communist or anything else. We all bleed red blood. I know. I saw plenty of blood on the battlefield. And the sad thing is the Nazis who died bled just the same as the Jews they tortured and the Allies they fought. We are all humans, all part of one family. Once people learn this it will be a better world."

"You think they ever gonna learn it?"

"I don't know. It's hard to say. Throughout history, there have always been wars and death for silly reasons. It's hate and fear. I can't honestly say whether mankind will ever conquer this, but I sure hope so."

CHAPTER THIRTY-FIVE

July 1965

At seven-thirty in the morning on July tenth, Haley Lynn Levi was born. Dovid and Eidel named her for Helen and Lars. Haley was smaller than her brother and sister and, unlike them, she was bald. Dovid thought she looked like a baby bird. Unlike Abby, who screamed, demanding what she wanted or Mark, who was always getting into things, Haley was quiet and not very active. She gave the appearance of being helpless and frightened like she somehow landed on earth by accident.

Eidel was different towards Haley than she'd been toward the other two, especially Abby. Haley brought out Eidel's protective instinct. Dovid didn't know if this was because he and Eidel had improved their relationship, or if it was because Haley was a different type of child. They brought her home from the hospital to find that she was completely undemanding to the point where Dovid was worried that something might be wrong with her. She slept through the night immediately, and wouldn't even cry if her diaper was wet or dirty. Eidel doted on Haley. Dovid had never seen her behave that way with either of the others. The more Haley lay quietly in her crib or on a blanket on the floor, the more Eidel picked the child up and held her close to her bosom.

As Haley got older, to Dovid's relief, he began to realize

that there was nothing wrong with Haley; she just had a very agreeable personality. In fact, she was a delight. She rarely cried. And after the first time she smiled, she began to laugh. Both Eidel and Dovid found her laughter to be so adorable that they were enchanted.

With three children, Eidel was overwhelmed. Ida still came over often, but she refused to take money for taking care of the children.

"If you won't take any money, I am going to have to hire someone to help me. I don't feel right about asking you to come here every day," Eidel said.

"I don't mind coming."

"I know. And I am always glad to see you. But I can't have you taking care of three small children."

"But we are doing it together," Ida said.

"Are you sure?"

"Of course, I am sure."

"Please, let me give you something?"

"Friends don't pay each other for things like this. Maybe you forget, Eidel. I can't have children of my own. The Nazis made sure of that. So Mark, Abby, and Haley are like my nieces and nephews. They satisfy my need to mother. I can shower them with love and gifts and it fulfills me. Does that make sense to you?"

"Yes, Ida. Of course it does."

"I have been trying not to come over every day so that you and Dovid could have your time alone together. But now with three little children, perhaps you need me?"

"Oh, yes, I do."

"Then I will be here. Don't you worry about that," Ida smiled and winked.

But Eidel was right. With Dovid home so much things between Eidel and Ida were different. As time passed, Eidel began to feel that she wasn't able to give Ida enough attention. It seemed like Ida was becoming more of a babysitter than a friend, and Eidel didn't want Ida to ever feel taken advantage of. Finally, the two women discussed the situation again and Ida reluctantly agreed that she would like it if Eidel hired a nanny to help her with the children. Ida had several things she wanted to do with her time, but as long as Eidel needed her, she would be there. However, now she would have more free time to fulfill some of her own dreams. The two women decided that Ida would only come by the Levi's house on the days when Dovid went in to work. That way, she and Eidel would have time together as lady friends without the presence of a man getting in the way.

Dovid and Eidel ran an ad in the job section of the newspaper, but Eidel could never find anyone she was comfortable with until Cool Breeze suggested a friend of his. Dovid and Eidel were sitting in the living room with the television on when Cool Breeze came in from downstairs. He was ready to leave for work.

"I heard you lookin' for somebody you can trust to helps you with the kids. I know's this gal. She a real nice gal, I tell you. And she sure could use the money. She be good with kids too. I think you would like her, Mrs. Eidel. Can I bring her by to meet you maybe on Sunday?"

"Sure," Dovid said, then he turned to Eidel. He could see that she was unsure by the look in her eyes. "Let's just meet her. I trust Cool Breeze's judgment."

"What's her name?" Eidel asked.

"Glory. She be a right good friend of mine," Cool Breeze smiled.

CHAPTER THIRTY-SIX

Cool Breeze and Dovid drove to the South Side on Sunday morning to pick up Glory. She was waiting outside of a tall apartment building when they arrived. Two men wearing berets leaned against the side of the building.

"Black Panthers?" Dovid asked Cool Breeze.

"Yes, that's what they be. They be a new gang," Cool Breeze answered as Glory got into the car. She was a tall, slender, spirited girl with a bright pretty smile.

"Glory, this be Mister Dovid. He my friend."

"Nice to meet you, sir," she said.

"Nice to meet you too. You can call me Dovid. No need for the sir."

"All right."

"So, Cool Breeze speaks highly of you. How do you two know each other?"

"I works part-time at the little general store on the corner right down the street from the tavern. But I sure would like a new job. Crawford say you be good to work for. He say you be kind and fair."

"Is that what he says? I've never heard anyone call him Crawford," Dovid laughed. "So," Dovid turned to Cool Breeze. "Is that what you say about me, Crawford?"

Cool Breeze laughed. "You the nicest white man I ever met.

In fact, you pretty close to the nicest fella I ever met."

When they got to Dovid's house, Dovid introduced Glory to Eidel and the children. When Glory lifted the children in her arms, even though they didn't know her, none of them cried. Not even Abby, who was the most difficult to please. Eidel and Glory talked for several minutes before Eidel nodded at Dovid. She smiled and then she hired Glory.

From the first time Dovid saw Glory and Cool Breeze together, he knew that they were dating. He could also tell that Cool Breeze was smitten with her. And it was easy to see why. She was at least ten years younger than Cool Breeze and exceptionally pretty. With deep brown eyes that slanted slightly, high cheekbones, processed hair, a light gloss of red lipstick, and matching nail polish, she looked more like a model than a nanny.

Glory fit in with the kids right away, and before long she became good friends with Eidel and Ida. On the days that Ida came to visit, the three women enjoyed several cups of coffee together. At first, Glory was shy and quiet around Eidel. But within a week, Glory's shell began to crack and she began to share her past with Eidel. She told Eidel how she had been born to a poor family in Alabama and how at twelve she had left her family home. With almost no money, she'd taken a bus to Chicago to live with her aunt who worked as a maid for a white family. Glory explained how she went to an all-white school and how uncomfortable she was being the only dark-skinned child.

"Childrens can be cruel. They turn a hard heart towards someone who is different than they are. I dropped out of school in the sixth grade. I wish'd I would a gone longer. Breeze said he went through the seventh grade then he had to drop out too. His reasons was different than mine though."

"That's not only children, Glory," Ida said. "I was in a concentration camp. The Germans were supposed to be the most civilized, educated, refined people in the world. But when the Nazis took over, the Nazis were heartless. They had methods of torture that could only be devised by the most terrible of monsters. My sister and I were experimented on, like lab rats, by an educated man. This man was a real doctor. He was so atrocious that he killed my dear beloved sister." A tear formed in the corner of Ida's eye, but she continued. "So it's not only children who can be cruel. It is anyone who feels threatened by someone who is different. Sadly, sometimes people feel that they must destroy what they are afraid to understand."

"My Sweet Jesus," Glory said shaking her head. "I heard tell of stories of slavery but this doctor tops it all."

"Slavery was a terrible thing too. Did you know that the Jews were slaves at one time too? Did you also know that it is against the Jewish religion to have slaves?" Ida said.

"I didn't know. So the Jews never had slaves?"

"They weren't supposed to. We believe that as long as anyone is suffering it is our responsibility as Jews to fight for them."

"Mrs. Eidel, was you in a camp too?" Glory asked.

"No. I would have been but my birth mother had me smuggled out of the Warsaw Ghetto before she was sent to a camp. I was brought up as a Catholic in Poland."

"You all has some stories too," Glory said.

"Yes, we do. That's why I never want you to feel that you

are different here. I want you to know that you are a part of our family. Both you and Cool Breeze work for us but you are not like employees, you're like relatives. I know my husband, Dovi, feels the same way. We both are so happy to have you here with us."

"Well, thank you, Mam. Thank you. It makes me feel good to know I's wanted."

"Eidel. Call me Eidel."

The family Glory's aunt had worked for allowed Glory to stay with them, but Glory was given strict instructions to stay out of their way.

"The less they saw of me, the better. It was like I was supposed to be invisible. Sometimes I feels like I ain't never had a chance to be a child."

"Well, that's all in the past now."

Eidel would have liked to offer Glory a place to stay at the Levi's house, but there was no room. Cool Breeze had been living in the basement and being that the two were not married, Eidel would never have suggested that Glory stay there with him. Eidel and Dovid slept in the master bedroom, Haley and Abby shared a room, and Mark had the other bedroom.

CHAPTER THIRTY-SEVEN

Ida loved her new-found freedom. She also relished the fact that she had a car and was able to drive. Even though she was all alone with Harry gone all evening, she was finally able to do as she pleased. Harry got home in the morning. He ate then he slept. While he was sleeping she took classes. Every day she made sure that she was at home by the time he awoke to prepare his dinner. He ate and was off to work by three in the afternoon. From that time on, she was free to go wherever she pleased. The Art Institute closed at five, but one afternoon she drove downtown to see it anyway. She only had an hour to explore the wonderful treasures, but it was well worth the drive. Another day she went to the Field Museum, where she saw a mummy and the bones of giant dinosaurs. Then, on another occasion, she took a ride on a train through the coal mines and experimented with the future of telephones at the Museum of Science and Industry. Occasionally, she stopped for dinner at small ethnic restaurants. It was as if she were seeing Chicago for the first time. The car had given her independence and she was enjoying every minute of it.

By the summer of 1966, Ida had a part-time job. She loved to cook and found work preparing authentic Polish dishes at a restaurant right outside downtown. To her excitement and surprise, the restaurant received a wonderful review in the food section of the Sun Sentinel. Ida's name was mentioned. The restaurant owner showed her the review, and then he hung it on the wall in front of the cash register. Ida felt like a celebrity when she saw her name on the printed page of a paper. Harry wasn't as pleased as Ida that she was out working at night.

"I'm doing well. I'm earning a decent living. Why do you need to do this?" he asked.

"I enjoy it? It keeps me busy?"

"But why do you want to drive all the way downtown?"

"Because that's where this restaurant is. They needed a Polish cook."

"How did you ever find it?"

"I saw a want ad in the job section of the newspaper. I can read English now, you know."

"Yes, you are thriving here in America." His voice took on a sarcastic edge.

"You sound like you don't like it that I am doing so well."

"It's not that, Ida. I just feel like I am losing you."

She shook her head. "Oh, Harry. We have been together for too long, and we've been through too much for you to lose me."

"But you meet so many other men ..."

"Yes, I do."

"And they probably try to ask you out."

"Sometimes, yes."

"And what if someday one comes along who you decide you like better than me?"

"Harry, I don't know what the future holds. All I know is that you have a life to live and I have one too. You are just going to have to take that chance because I am not quitting my job."

He looked at her then shook his head. "You are one stubborn woman, Ida."

"I suppose I am, but I think it's what kept me alive, Harry. I refused to give up even when I saw my sister die, and I refuse to sit at home and wait for you to get off of work, paralyzed with fear of living life to its fullest. I cannot promise you that I will never leave you. Nobody can honestly say that they know what the future will bring. You could leave me someday. It could happen," she said.

He shook his head. "Never," he said.

"Harry, Harry, Harry. You are one special man. But, let's face it; we can never be sure of anything. But what I can tell you is this … right now, at this moment in time, as we stand here in our kitchen … I love you and I have no intention of going anywhere without you."

"Even after all these years of marriage, Ida, you keep me on my toes. Maybe that's why I'm so crazy about you."

She kissed him. "Let's make love before you have to go in to work," she said.

CHAPTER THIRTY-EIGHT

By the winter of 1967, Cool Breeze and Glory were engaged to be married. Cool Breeze asked Dovid to teach him to drive. It was a fiasco that took all of Dovid's patience. Dovid had to help him improve his reading skills as well as his driving ability so he would be able to pass the written test. But, after several weeks, Cool Breeze, with the excitement of a child, finally got his license. Dovid drove Cool Breeze to a used car dealership where Cool Breeze bought his first car.

"I suppose Glory and me should be thinkin' about getting a place of our own," Cool Breeze said. "Or at least payin' you some kind of rent. I been livin' here rent-free for years. Now when Glory and me gets hitched, we both gonna be livin' here? It ain't right. I owes you something."

"Are you happy living here with us, Cool Breeze?" Dovid asked.

"Of course, who wouldn't be happy? I got me a nice apartment with tile floors and a clean bathroom with a sink, a tub, and a toilet, right there by my bedroom not down no hall the way they got it in a flophouse. But sometimes, I feels bad, like I should be payin' you some kinda rent."

"No need. If I ever need any money from you, I'll let you know. Now, let's talk about your wedding," Dovid said.

"Ain't nothin' to talk about. Glory gonna invite her aunt. I don't speak to none of my brothers. Wouldn't even know where to find em. My Ma and Pa long dead. So, it's just us."

"Well, then, I'll take everyone out for dinner," Dovid said. "We'll invite Ida and Harry, and we'll all go downtown to the Blackhawk steak house. The only problem is … a babysitter," Dovid said.

"I have an idea," Cool Breeze said. "Why don't we bring in food? That way we can take the kids to the courthouse for the wedding, and then we can all come back here to the house to celebrate."

"You think Glory would like that?"

"Yeah, she be so grateful to you folks for all you done for us."

Dovid smiled. "I am blessed, Cool Breeze. I don't know how or why, but God has seen fit to give me plenty of money. It is my pleasure to be able to share it with those I care about. You and Harry are my best friends."

"You got a good heart, Dovi Levi. You sure 'nough do."

CHAPTER THIRTY-NINE

February 1968

Not much changed after Cool Breeze and Glory were married. Glory moved into the basement. Then one day she surprised everyone. In accordance with the new hairstyles, she let her hair go natural.

"It's called a fro. Do you like it?" she asked Eidel.

"It's big," Eidel said. "And full."

"This is the way my hair looks when it's not processed."

"What is processed?"

"You remember how my hair was flat but wavy before?"

"Yes, of course."

"Well, it took my hairdresser hours to get it to look like that. She had to straighten it with some stinky, burning chemicals, then press it with hot irons. Sometimes, if she wasn't quick enough, it would burn off. The way that you be seein' my hair right now is the way it is when it's natural. For years, black women was trying to look as white as they could. So, they would go and have a process done to make their hair look more like white women hair. Now, we tryin' hard to make folks see that black is beautiful and black womens can be beautiful just they way God made 'em."

"I think this is a good thing, Glory. You are a beautiful woman, no matter how you wear your hair," Eidel said.

Cool Breeze drove to work with Harry every day. They shared the driving. On Sunday, all three couples enjoyed dinner together. Sometimes they discussed the changes they were seeing in the world.

"We don't use the word colored no more, it's offensive. It makes us feel like we one step above slaves. Now we call ourselves black folks," Cool Breeze said. "It's part of this here new movement with Dr. King. He tryin' hard to give us pride in our black heritage. Lots of white folks don't like him. They think he makin' us too uppity."

"I like him, Cool Breeze. I believe that this is what the black man in America needs. And I also believe in my heart that one day there will be a black president of this great country because the black man is a big part of this great land. I hope it happens in my lifetime."

"Ain' it just like you, Mister Dovi, to say that. Sometimes I think you one of the best folks I ever knowd."

"Come on, stop it. You and I both know that King is right. I am not one of the best men in the world. I am only being fair. I have plenty of faults but one thing I pride myself on and that is being fair."

Cool Breeze nodded.

CHAPTER FORTY

On the fourth of April at six o'clock in the evening, Dr. Martin Luther King stood on the balcony of his hotel room in Memphis, Tennessee. He looked out across the city; Jesse Jackson stood at his side. They had come to conduct a peaceful march with a group of sanitation workers who were on strike.

We are making progress, Dr. King thought, but the black man still has a long way to go before he is recognized as an equal. I intend to devote the rest of my life to bringing about a peaceful union between all of mankind.

As Dr. King surveyed the people and activity on the streets below him, a shot was fired from a 30-caliber rifle. The bullet seemed to come out of nowhere. It entered King's jaw and then went on to pierce his jugular vein. A waterfall of blood poured from the wound.

An hour later, Dr. King died at St. Joseph's Hospital. This was the end of peace. The leader of the black movement, who had a dream of love and people joining together in a world of equality and light, was gone. In the wake of his death came anger, violence, and terrible riots in the streets of all the major cities. One of the worst occurred in the city of Chicago, which was under the jurisdiction of Mayor Richard J. Daley. First came the looting of all the local businesses in the black areas of the city followed by fighting and shootings. Then angry mobs ran through the areas, setting everything on fire as they passed. Mayor Daley was not going to surrender the city. He came on television and said that he'd told the police to "Shoot to kill...shoot to maim." Chicago became a war zone between the blacks, the white business owners, and the police. Mayhem, destruction, and murders followed.

CHAPTER FORTY-ONE

Cool Breeze was popping the top off of a beer bottle when Dovid came rushing into the bar.

"Did you see the news?" he asked Cool Breeze.

"Been too busy."

Before Dovid had a chance to say another word a big metal trash can came flying through the window. A shard of glass soared through the air and cut Harry on the cheek.

"What the hell?" Harry said, ducking behind the food counter.

There was a roar of shouting as crowds of people grew larger outside.

"We have to close and get out of here," Dovid said loud enough for both Harry and Cool Breeze to hear. Then he addressed the patrons. "Listen to me, we are closing. It's time to leave. Go home. Hurry, get out of the streets."

But there wasn't time to leave. A band of looters came in. They were carrying guns.

"Gimme all the whiskey," one of them said to Cool Breeze.

"You can't carry all them bottles." Cool Breeze looked at the young black man wearing a beret. "You be a Black Panther?" he asked.

"Yes. I am a Black Panther, and you're an uncle Tom. You work for whitey. YOU kiss whitey's ass."

"It ain't like that. I be the manager here. This be my place you in."

"You don't own it. Whitey takes advantage of you. He works you to death while he makes all the money."

"That's where you're wrong young man. You don't know nothin' bout the owner of this place. He be good to me. He be good to black folks."

"You just a brainwashed fool," the Black Panther said, pointing a gun at Cool Breeze. "I said give me the whiskey, boy."

"Give it to him," Dovid said.

"Who the hell are you, whitey?"

"I'm Dovid Levi. I own this place. Cool Breeze is my friend."

The Black Panther turned the gun on Dovid. "You the owner? You the white owner?"

"That's right," Dovid said.

Cool Breeze began pulling down all the bottles of whiskey and putting them on the bar. "Here, don't hurt nobody, just take what you wants and go."

Just then Glory walked in. Cool Breeze's mouth dropped open. "What you doin' here baby? You should be at the house. Why you come down here in the middle all this trouble?"

"That your girl?" the Black Panther asked. "Ain't she a pretty little thing." He touched her hair. "You know your man is an Uncle Tom? You know he kisses whitey's ass?"

"You don't know nothin' about us. You don't know nothin'

about Mister Dovi either. You just an angry kid. Don't think I don't feel real bad about what happened to Dr. King. I loved him too. But, what you doin' by rioting ain't gonna bring him back. And I can tell you this for sure, Dr. King wouldn't approve of all this shit you and your friends are…" Glory said her hands on her hips in defiance.

"Shut up, you stupid bitch."

"Don't talk to her that way. I won't have it. This is still my bar. And whether you have a gun or not, you are still on my property. I am not scared of you. If you want to prove you're a man put the gun down and let's fight fair. Can you fight with fists? Go ahead and show me what you've got," Dovid said, straightening his back and looking right into the Black Panther's eyes.

"It don't matter, mister Dovi," Glory said. She was trembling. "Please don't fight him."

"I ain't gonna fight you old man. I'm gonna shoot you." The Black Panther pointed the gun at Dovi. Dovi didn't move. He stood staring into the man's eyes.

"Don't," Glory said. As the Black Panther was about to pull the trigger, Glory threw herself in front of Dovid.

The bullet ripped right into her chest. Glory let out a gasp as she crumbled to the floor in a pool of blood. The group that was with the Black Panther took the bottles of whiskey and walked outside. But as they were leaving, one of them threw a Molotov cocktail into the gap in the broken window. A massive explosion followed. It rocked the building and within minutes the entire bar was engulfed in flames.

Cool Breeze lifted Glory in his arms. Dovid helped him. Harry followed and the three of them got out to the street.

Police cars were everywhere. Dovid ran up to the first one he could find.

"Help us, please help us. Someone has been shot. She needs to get to the hospital right away."

CHAPTER FORTY-TWO

Dovid and Harry stayed at Cool Breeze's side as they sat outside the emergency room. They were waiting for the doctor to come out of the examining room and tell them how Glory was doing. The smell of rubbing alcohol and the sight of doctors with stethoscopes brought back memories of Dovid's father.

"Are you Mr. Dell?" a young doctor with wavy brown hair and calm eyes asked Cool Breeze.

Cool Breeze nodded.

"I'm sorry, Mr. Dell. We did all we could."

Glory Marie Washington Dell was pronounced dead at 4:30 a.m. that morning.

Cool Breeze made a sound like an animal choking. Then he looked down at the floor.

"Will you be taking care of the arrangements?" the doctor asked in a soft voice.

"Ain't gonna be no arrangements. She got no family, and she and me aint got no money saved. I guess you gonna have to do whatever it is you do when this kind of thing happen."

Dovid could see that Cool Breeze was having a hard time holding back his tears. For the first time since he'd met him, he could see that Cool Breeze was angry.

"I'll pay for a plot and a coffin," Dovid said.

"You ain't gotta do that Mister Dovid."

"I want to," Dovid said. Then he turned to the doctor and said, "I'll be in touch with you."

Dovid took Cool Breeze's arm and the three men walked outside. It wasn't exceptionally cold for April, but Cool Breeze was shivering.

"You two go on home," Cool Breeze said. "I need to walk for a while. Gotta take some time and be by myself. I'll be getting' on back to the house in a bit."

"Are you sure?" Dovid asked. He was worried about letting Cool Breeze go off alone in his condition.

Cool Breeze didn't answer. He just turned and began to walk away.

Dovid and Harry stood watching Cool Breeze until he disappeared into the darkness and then they went home.

Cool Breeze didn't return that night or the following morning. The riots in the streets of Chicago continued. Although Eidel begged Dovid to stay at home, he was too worried about Cool Breeze. He didn't tell Eidel where he was going or why, but, Dovid got dressed and drove right into the heart of the war zone in search of his friend. He rode past the tavern; it was burnt to the ground. A few feet away from the building, the sign that said "Arnie's Little Slice 'O Heaven" lay broken into pieces. Dovid felt sick because he knew something that no one else knew yet. Dovid had just lost everything he had. It was a stupid mistake. Dovid had been meaning to get insurance but had kept putting it off. Now it was too late. All he had left was his house and a small savings. Harry, too, would be affected by Dovid's mistake and Dovid felt terrible about it. But, right at that very moment

164

in time, all of that was not as important as the fact that he couldn't find Cool Breeze anywhere. He went to the flophouse but the restaurant where Harry had once worked was now dark and Dovid had no idea where to begin to search. Still, he kept driving. Then, at two that afternoon, he passed a large building on fire. It was surrounded by an angry mob. When the mob saw Dovi they surrounded his car. Some of the men began banging their fists on the windshield. Dovid's heart leaped out of his chest.

What am I going to do? I can't run these people over with my car. But if one of them grabs an object large enough to break the window, I am done for. Or even worse, if one of them has a gun ...

Then Dovid got an idea.

Thank God it's a windy night.

He always had a roll of dollar bills in his pocket. Since he'd started working at the bar he made it a habit to keep a wad of singles on his person in case he needed to make change. Dovid pulled the money out of his pants pocket and cracked the window. He separated the bills and threw them out the window. The hearty breeze that came off Lake Michigan took the paper currency and flung it all over the street. The mob went after the money. They began grabbing whatever they could get. Fights ensued. There was utter chaos. But during the confusion, they forgot about Dovid and he saw his way out. As soon as the road was clear enough for him to maneuver through, Dovid quickly sped away.

Tired, depressed, and not sure where else to look for Cool Breeze, Dovid headed home. Eidel was awake, waiting for him.

"Did Cool Breeze come home or did he call?"

" Actually come to think of it, I haven't seen him or Glory. But, you know how he is. He comes in late, sometimes he leaves early. He often takes Glory with him. I just didn't realize that they weren't here. I guess I was too worried about you to pay much attention to anything else." Eidel said

"Oh, my sweetheart. I'm fine." Dovid said. *She has no idea.*

"You want something to eat? Or something to drink?"

"I'll get myself a whiskey," Dovid said.

"You hardly ever drink alcohol," Eidel rubbed Dovid's shoulder.

"I can't find Cool Breeze. I hope he's all right."

"Yes, so do I."

"Do you want a drink, Eidel?"

She let out a short laugh. "You know … I have never tasted whiskey."

"Here, let me pour you a little. I have something to tell you. I've been avoiding telling you because it is terrible. Terrible. And I know how sensitive you are sometimes. Maybe, the whiskey might help." His hands were trembling. He had waited as long as he could to give her the bad news. She had to know. Sooner or later she had to know.

Eidel took a sip. "Wheew that burns."

"Yes, it does. Sometimes it burns away the pain of life."

"What is it, Dovi?"

"There is so much I have to say …"

"NU? So say it, please…you're making me nervous."

"Glory was killed last night."

"Killed? My God, Dovi …" Eidel put her face in her hands. "How? What happened?"

"She was protecting me."

"You?"

"Yes, me. Then after she died, Cool Breeze was so distraught that he couldn't come right home. He insisted on going for a walk alone. I haven't heard from him since. The riots that we have been watching on TV are worse than you could imagine. It's like a war is going on right in the streets."

"Killed? My God! Poor Glory. Poor Cool Breeze. Thank God you're home safe. Is Harry all right?"Eidel got up and rubbed Dovid's shoulders hard as if she were holding onto him fearing that she might lose him to death too.

He nodded. "Yes, Harry is fine. But I don't know what happened to Cool Breeze. I don't even know where to begin to look for him. And it's not safe to go down to the tavern."

She shook her head.

"And, Eidel … about the tavern … they burned it to the ground."

"Burned it?" She was in shock. He could see it in her face. It was a lot of terrible news all at once, but he had to tell her the truth. He couldn't keep it a secret even though he wanted to. She had to know.

"We had no insurance. We can't rebuild the bar. I guess what I am trying to tell you is …we aren't rich anymore," Dovid said.

Eidel lifted the glass of whiskey and downed it entirely in one swig. Her head shook involuntarily from the strength of the drink. Then she was silent for a moment. Clearing her throat and taking both of his hands she gazed intently into his eyes. "We'll manage. We always have. As long as we have each other, we'll survive this."

CHAPTER FORTY-THREE

Dovid called Harry the following day and told him that he needed to speak with him and Ida. He knew he had to give Harry the bad news about the loss of the tavern, but he couldn't bring himself to tell him on the phone. Harry and Ida said they would come by in the morning.

Harry brought bagels, lox, and cream cheese. Dovid felt sick. He couldn't eat. How was he ever going to tell his friends that not only had his negligence ruined his own family, but it had destroyed their livelihood as well?

Dovid was silent as he watched Harry help the women set up the food on the kitchen table. The TV was on, playing softly. Although no one was actually watching it, they could hear news about the riots still going on in the background. Eidel knew how hard this was going to be for Dovid. She finished helping Ida and Harry then she went into the living room where Dovid was looking out the window.

"Come, Dovi, eat. Then we'll tell them together. It will be all right."

Eidel put her hand on her husband's shoulder. He was amazed at the inner strength he saw in her. He had always thought of Eidel as weak and delicate but in his time of need she was showing him a side of her he had never seen. All the love he'd always felt for her was burning in the tears that threatened to spill from his eyes. The sound of an angry mob, shouting and breaking glass in the background, came from the television.

Dovid sat down beside Eidel. Everyone ate, the delicious fragrance of brewing coffee filled the air.

"Harry, I'm sorry. I failed you," Dovid said. He sighed. "We've lost the bar. We've lost everything. I drove by there yesterday, it's burned to the ground."

"We can rebuild," Harry said looking concerned.

"There was no insurance. There is no money to rebuild."

"What about the land? Can we sell the land and start over somewhere else?" Harry asked.

Dovid shook his head. "We don't own the land. We paid rent on it. This is all my fault. I should have had the place insured. I just didn't take the time to take care of it and now ..."

"What about Cool Breeze? Have you heard anything from Cool Breeze?"

"Not a word."

"So what are we going to do now?" Harry said.

"I don't know. I am so stunned that I'm numb. I feel sick with guilt for what I've done to you and Ida."

Ida stood up and walked over to the TV. She turned it off. "No sense in sitting and watching this. We already know what is happening on the South Side. Now we have to figure out what we are going to do to ensure our future. Harry and I have a little money saved."

"We have some as well," said Eidel.

"I have built a good name for myself in the restaurant

business," Ida said. "I think maybe we should go in together and open a small Polish restaurant in downtown Skokie. Oakton Street looks like a promising location. There are a lot of shops opening there. There should be plenty of traffic. We can post all of the reviews from the newspapers about my cooking right in the window. I have met a few Chicago restaurant critics. I will try to contact them and see if they will come in and give us a try. If they write good reviews we can build our business on their recommendations. What do you two think about this idea?"

"I think you're a genius!" Eidel said.

Dovid nodded. "I think it's a good idea."

"Yes, me too," Harry agreed.

CHAPTER FORTY-FOUR

Even with their future so uncertain, and knowing that he should save every penny, Dovid still bought a plot in the cemetery next to the two plots he'd already purchased for himself and Eidel. He arranged for Glory's burial, as he had promised Cool Breeze he would.

Harry, Ida, Dovid, and Eidel were there as they laid Glory to rest, but Cool Breeze never came.

I hope he's not dead. I pray he didn't kill himself.

Dovid felt that Harry was thinking the same thing, but neither said a word.

After the funeral, both couples went back to Dovid's house.

On April seventh, the riots in Chicago ended, leaving eleven dead, five hundred injured, and over two thousand people arrested.

CHAPTER FORTY-FIVE

July 1968

Ida searched up and down Oakton Street until she found a storefront for rent. She called everyone she'd ever met in the restaurant business until she found someone who had used equipment that they wanted to sell. She met with the seller and negotiated until she got a fair deal on everything she needed to open the restaurant. Next, Ida and Eidel scanned resale stores all over the city until they found an eclectic blend of twelve sets of tables and chairs.

Together, the two couples cleaned the store. They painted and washed down the big picture windows. Eidel scrubbed the bathroom until it shone.

Harry went to thrift stores where he bought used sets of dishes and silverware.

Finally, they set a date for a grand opening.

Every night Ida came to the Levis' house and she and Ida baked soft, braided challah bread from scratch as well as an array of delectable desserts for the restaurant. Harry acted as a host and waiter, and he also bussed the tables. Eidel was in charge of taking the money. They still didn't have a cash register, so all transactions were made out of a metal box.

At first, things were very slow. Dovid was worried; he had invested every penny that he'd saved and if the restaurant didn't make it then he would have to start over with nothing.

Dovid and Ida were in charge of the cooking. They used most of Ida's recipes. The food was delicious, and the prices were reasonable. Since Skokie was populated by a large number of eastern European Jews, many of whom had survived the Nazis and come to America, Ida's home cooking was a wonderful reminder of their lives before Hitler. When a customer walked into Ida's they could smell the glorious aroma of real homemade Matzo ball soup and kreplach. Once in a while, Dovid would notice a customer wiping away a tear and he thought that maybe the fragrance had probably brought back memories.

But word of mouth was slow, and people didn't go out to dinner much during the week. Unlike the tavern, which had been busy six days a week, the restaurant did most of its business on the weekends. It was difficult to know how much food to order and often there was a lot of spoilage and waste.

The two couples sat down after the restaurant closed one night and talked about their situation.

"I think I should look for a job in the city while the two of you work the restaurant," Dovid said. "Eidel can stay at home with the children. As you know, we had to hire a nanny and that is costing more than we are earning. Unfortunately, there just isn't enough money coming in from the restaurant to support two families. I will try to earn enough to take care of my family and for now, you two take whatever the restaurant brings in. But as soon as business picks up, we can all come back to work here."

"You think it will ever pick up?" Harry asked.

"I hope so. But for now, I think it's best that I look for

174

work."

And so Dovid began searching for a job as a bartender. He went from tavern to tavern throughout the city. He had plenty of experience. But, even so, it wasn't as easy as he had anticipated. For three months he went out on interviews every day, but no one hired him.

By December, money was really tight. Dovid had a family to feed and a mortgage. He sold the car and he and Eidel began taking buses, which were not as reliable in the suburbs as they were in the city. All three children were growing quickly but there was no money for new shoes or clothes. Eidel took the children to a thrift store where she bought them what she could. In January of 1969, Eidel decided to take the L train into the heart of downtown and try to get work. She spent three weeks going to shops, offices, and restaurants, hoping to find any kind of a job. While she was gone she left the children at the restaurant with Ida but she returned home each night defeated.

There was almost nothing left now. Dovid began shoveling snow for neighbors to earn a few dollars. However, it was hardly enough for a family to survive on. The children were living on boiled white rice, noodles, and cans of beans. What was left of their savings was almost completely gone, and once it was, Dovid knew that they would no longer be able to pay the mortgage. That summer, Dovid mowed lawns, trimmed trees, and did odd jobs. He went hungry to feed the children and somehow he was able to keep paying the mortgage.

If I had only known what I know now, I would have paid for this house in full when I had the money. I never saw this coming.

Harry and Ida weren't doing any better at the restaurant.

Finally, by the summer of 1970, there was no more money left in either Harry's or Dovid's savings accounts. The two couples got together at Dovid's house to talk things over.

"I'm not ready to give up on the restaurant," Ida said.

"The restaurant is just making its own bills," Harry said. "We are going to have to put the house up for sale."

"Yes, we are as well," Eidel said. "I talked to a real estate agent last week."

"You never told me," Dovid said.

"I know. I didn't want it to come to this. But I think we are going to have to sell, Dovi."

Dovid nodded.

Eidel took care of everything with the realtor. But when Dovid saw the "For Sale" sign outside his house, he felt sick to his stomach. Even worse, he hadn't been able to find any odd jobs for a while and because of it he had no money to buy food. The children were hungry. Mark was eight, Abby seven, and Haley turning six. They were too young to understand their parents' problems. Dovid chastised himself as he watched them suffering for his stupid mistake. Mark and Abby were embarrassed to go to school wearing used clothes. They complained to their parents and cried about not fitting in. They wanted penny loafers like the other kids but Dovid could not buy them the shoes everyone else had and he felt even more like a failure. The children took peanut butter sandwiches to school for lunch each day, and somehow Dovid managed to be sure that he was able to provide at least that much. Many nights, Dovid said he wasn't hungry and he didn't eat in order to make sure that there was enough for the children and Eidel. Eidel, too, secretly saved her portion for the children. When Dovid looked at his kids he felt that they looked unhealthy. They needed some meat or fresh vegetables. But how was he ever to acquire these things without any money? When there was produce left over at the restaurant Ida gave it to the Levi's for the children. But often there was nothing left. Never telling anyone what he was doing, Dovid began to pick the spoiling produce out of the garbage behind the local grocery store. He washed it well and cut off the rotten parts, then gave it to Eidel to make soup. She never asked him where he got the vegetables or why they were cut up. She quite simply boiled water and prepared a soup. Dovid refused to give up. Every week he continued to look for work, taking the L into the city. He also spent days applying at local factories, but still nothing. Dovid was a fighter but failure had made him feel the heaviness of defeat and he began to walk with his shoulders slumped and his head down.

There has to be a job I can get. There must be something that I can do for work. There must be something I am missing? Some stone I've left unturned, he thought, but he could think of nothing.

And then came the winter of 1971. It was a chilly day in early January. The house had been up for sale for a long time, but there had been no offers. The restaurant was doing a little better. It was paying its own bills and both mortgages, but just barely. If the house didn't sell and the restaurant couldn't pay, the Levis would be evicted and Dovid would have to move his family into a cheap apartment in the city. And, truth be told, if things continued the way they were going, he wouldn't even be able to afford that. All three children were sick with colds. Dovid blamed himself for that too. After all, he was not heating the house properly.

Arnie, what would you think of me now? I am so ashamed. My

177

kids need better food. Eidel should be able to make them chicken soup but she can't. There is no money for chicken. Arnie, what the hell am I going to do?

Then, Dovid got an idea. He hated himself for what he was about to do, but he knew he must do it. The family kept rags that had once been baby clothes under the kitchen sink. Dovid cut the fabric into squares. Then he made pockets on the inside of his winter coat. Sewing them carefully, he then tested them to make sure they were strong enough to hold two cans of beans.

Next, he put on his coat and walked several blocks in a blizzard to the grocery store. Dovid was resorting to the unthinkable in order to provide for his family. On that day, Dovid Levi, knowing his parents would be filled with shame, began stealing food. He did it only when there was no other possible way to acquire food, and he never took more than he needed. But if he was unable to find odd jobs, then once a week he would take a chicken or a block of cheese. Occasionally, he would come back and get a box of noodles or rice. Eidel never asked where the food came from but he was sure she knew. After all, she hung up his coat and never questioned why he'd sewn pockets into it. He was grateful for her love, but when he looked into her eyes he was terribly ashamed.

By the end of March, the weather had become too warm for Dovid to be wearing a heavy coat but he needed to take a block of cheese for the children's dinner. A lighter jacket would be pulled down by the weight of the cheese. He didn't know what else to do. So, he wore the heavy coat and slipped the block of cheese into the inside pocket. Dovid swallowed hard and began to leave the store quickly but as he walked out the owner followed and stopped him.

"YOU, come with me," the grocery store owner said, grabbing Dovid's sleeve. Everyone in the store turned around to look. Dovid had never been so mortified in all of his life. Neighbors who knew the Levis stared at him with surprised looks that quickly turned to disgust. Dovid didn't care if he went to jail, all he could think of was his children and how they would be ostracized at school when the gossip began to spread about what he had done that day.

Once the grocery store owner and Dovid were alone, the man asked Dovid to empty his pockets.

Dovid began to comply, but the man didn't give him a chance to finish. Instead, the grocer reached into Dovid's coat and pulled out the cheese.

"One of my employees saw you steal this," the man said, picking up the round orange circle covered in wax.

"I'm sorry," Dovid said, looking down at the floor. He felt sick to his stomach.

"Why would you steal? You're a grown man, what makes a grown man steal? I am going to assume this is not your first time. Is it? Don't lie to me."

"No, it's not. I have stolen from you before. I am sure you will find it hard to believe me but I am an honest man. I never wanted to do this."

"Then why in God's name did you?"

"I have three children. I can't get a job. I swear to you that I never give up looking for work of any kind; I never stop trying. Every day I go out searching but so far I have been unsuccessful. I am the father of my family, the man of the house. Taking care of my wife and children is my responsibility no matter what I must do. I had no other way of

179

providing for them … so I stole. You can put me in jail for this. I am aware of it. But my children and wife need me. If you let me go, I promise you that, as soon as I am able, I will pay you every penny for the food I have taken from you," Dovid said, choking on the words.

The store owner looked at Dovid then his shoulders slumped, and he said, "I'm not going to call the police. Take the cheese and get out of here. But don't come back."

"Thank you," Dovid said. "I promise you, I will pay you everything I owe you."

The ground in the parking lot was filled with gray slush where the ice and snow had begun melting. The sun was beginning to set. While Dovid had been in the store, the temperature had dropped at least ten degrees and it was cold. Dovid waded through the half-frozen water and sunk down on the bench at the bus stop. He felt the frigid wind whip across his face and the chill made him feel the depth of his humiliation even more greatly. There was no one around, so Dovid started to speak aloud.

Arnie, I wish you were here to tell me what to do. I can't find any work. I am out of money. My children are going to starve. What should I do, Arnie? I am not lazy. I would clean bathrooms, sweep floors. I've tried everything to get a job and no one will hire me. You were like a papa to me. In fact, you were closer to me than my own papa whom I hardly remember. What should I do Arnie? What should I do? Something has to break or my wife and my children are going to be living in a shelter.

A tear slid down his face. He wiped it with his sleeve.

Dovid decided it was foolish to waste even a quarter. He would save the bus fare and walk home. As he walked it grew darker outside and chillier. His eyelashes froze, and his toes grew numb, but he still continued on foot toward home.

How does a man go from being a wealthy, successful businessman to taking his family to live in a flophouse? Dear God, I don't care what happens to me but please, I am begging you, for Eidel and my kids. Please, you must show me a way to provide. I can't take them to the flophouse to live and feed them from the soup kitchens.

Dovid passed the Synagogue where he had been a member before he lost the tavern. He'd given up the membership when he could no longer afford to pay his dues. His mind retraced the memory of the day he and Eidel had joined the temple. Dovid had been happy to give a substantial donation in honor of his parents that day. The rabbi had been kind and grateful for his generosity. Dovid had always meant to go to Shul at least on Saturday, but he had always been too busy.

Maybe I should have gone. I wanted to go, more for community than for religion. But it just never seemed like the right time. And then, well, I wasn't a member anymore. Maybe if I had visited God's house more often, he would have taken the time to give me an answer now, Dovid thought. Then he realized that God was sending him an answer.

Dovid's face was hot with embarrassment but he still walked through the heavy door of Temple Beth Israel. Inside, one of the last rays of sunlight beamed through a stained glass window, leaving a pattern of vivid color on the blond hardwood floor. The warmth of the heater caressed his face and hands. As Dovid stood wiping his feet on a mat by the front door, a young woman with dark hair, wrapped in a French twist, came up to him.

"Can I help you?"

"If you please … I would like to see Rabbi Mittleman."

"Do you have an appointment?"

"No, I am sorry, I don't. Is he busy? Shall I make an appointment?" Dovid felt suddenly foolish for having come into the temple to see the rabbi at all.

It's too late to back out now. I can't let pride get in the way of caring for my loved ones.

"Let me go and ask him if he can see you. What is your name?"

"Dovid Levi."

"Come into my office and have a seat. I'll be right back," the pretty young woman said. Dovid followed the woman into a small office and sat down. He waited almost ten minutes during which he wished he could run away. But even though he was uncomfortable with what he was about to do, he had to stay. He had to do this for his family.

Rabbi Mittleman was an older man. Dovid assumed probably in his late seventies. His thinning gray hair was neatly combed and he wore a clean white long sleeve shirt with baggy black pants.

"Dovid Levi!" The rabbi said, extending his hand for Dovid to shake. "It's been a long time."

"Yes, Rabbi. It has."

"Well, it certainly is good to see you. Come, we'll go into my office. Can I offer you a cup of coffee and a pastry perhaps?"

"Thank you, that would be very nice," Dovid said, wishing he could wrap the pastry in a napkin and bring it home for the children to share. Of course, he knew he couldn't do that in front of the rabbi. But he wished he could.

"Rachel, would you mind bringing us two cups of coffee and a tray of pastries, please?" The rabbi turned to the young woman.

"Of course, Rabbi."

Rachel returned with a tray of coffee and pastries that she set down on the table.

"Anything else I can do for you, Rabbi?" she asked.

"No, thank you. Please close the door when you go."

Rachel left, Dovid and the rabbi were alone. Rabbi Mittleman looked at Dovid with the kind eyes of a father who had experienced plenty of pain and said, "What brings you to me today, Dovid?"

Dovid told him. He told him everything ... about the loss of his business, the inability to find work. Then he began to weep when he admitted to stealing food. The rabbi sat quietly and listened.

"I hope you won't look down on me for the things I've done," Dovid said, staring at the floor.

"I have faced plenty of tragedy in my life. In fact, you know what? I too have stolen food."

"You, Rabbi?"

"Oh yes, it was long ago. But I will never forget." The rabbi pulled up his sleeve to reveal a crude tattoo of blue numbers on his forearm. "I was in a concentration camp. I needed food to live. I took what I could steal. I don't look down on you, Dovid."

"What can I do, Rabbi? How can I take care of my family? Tell me and I'll do whatever you say."

"It just so happens, Dovid Levi, that I need a custodian here at the temple. It would be a perfect job for you. Would you like it?"

"Oh yes. Oh, thank you, Rabbi ... God bless you, Rabbi."

"You need a job. I need a good man. It will work out well for both of us. Go home now. Get some rest. You'll start work tomorrow. But before you leave, why don't you wrap up these pastries and take them home for your children. I know how much children enjoy sweets. And I am getting too fat. So it's better if they are not sitting around here. When they're here I eat them," the rabbi said, winking. Then he got up and patted Dovid on the shoulder.

"Are you sure, Rabbi?"

"Of course, I am sure. Use the napkins." The rabbi smiled. Then he left the room.

And so it was that Dovid began working as a custodian at Temple Beth Israel. Several months later, when the young woman who was the rabbi's secretary decided to go back to college, the rabbi asked Dovid if he knew of anyone who could type and do mailings for him part-time. With all three children in school most of the day, Eidel was free to take the job. The rabbi hired her. And so, between what Dovid earned and Eidel earned they were able to keep their home. Ida and Harry sold their house, but they kept the restaurant open. It made just enough money for them to rent a small apartment above the restaurant.

CHAPTER FORTY-SIX

July 1972

The Levis still didn't earn enough money to purchase an automobile; they used public transportation. However, even with all he had lost, Dovid was grateful to God that the family had been able to keep their home and that there was enough food on the table each night. The Levi children didn't have all the material things that their classmates had, and many times Dovid would see envy on his children's faces when one of their friends received a new toy. Dovid wished he could give them everything in the world. However, he couldn't, so he did what he was able to do in order to make their lives better. If someone was looking for a handyman to fix a faucet or shovel snow, Dovid was always willing to do the work. He would then put the extra money toward things the children needed. But, sometimes, he would splurge and buy something for Eidel. Something he knew would make her smile. And, even after all these years together, her smile could still light up his world. For Hanukkah every year, each child received new shoes, one pair of pajamas, and a few pairs of underwear. If it was at all financially possible, Dovid tried to get them each a small toy to open on the eighth and final night. He loved to see them excited with anticipation.

When Mark turned nine, he had two friends from school over for birthday cake. Dovid went to a resale store where he negotiated a deal on a used bicycle, which he bought for Mark. But when he gave it to Mark, he showed no interest in the bike.

"Don't you like it?" Dovid asked.

Mark just shrugged.

Dovid was worried about his son, who refused to play any sports and had no interest in learning to ride the bike. Dovid knew that when the boys in the neighborhood went to the park to play football, Mark stayed inside. He was not a popular boy. He spent most of his time alone in his room. However, he did have one thing he truly loved—the theater. Several days a week, Mark would stay after school to be a part of the drama club. And it was there that he excelled. He made a couple of close friends and these two came to his birthday party. One was a scrawny girl with thin, stringy blond hair and a wonderful singing voice and the other was Earl Shulman. At nine years old, Earl was already handsome; he could sing like Frank Sinatra and dance like Fred Astaire. When Mark's elementary school put on a production, Mark was always a part of the cast but Earl was always the lead. After rehearsal, Earl would come to the Levi's home to spend time with Mark. Sometimes, Dovid could hear Mark singing songs from Broadway musicals.

I should have gotten him a record player and some records. I got him a bike because it's what I would have wanted as a kid. But, let's face it. I knew it was not something he would like, Dovid thought.

I was just hoping that if I got it for him he would ride it. I just can't help worrying about that boy. Something isn't quite right with him. What am I going to do if my only son is a fagel? That would be a father's nightmare. What a rough life Mark would have if he liked boys instead of girls. Oy, God forbid.

186

As Mark grew up, Dovid felt that they were growing more and more apart. Something about Mark scared his father. Every day, Dovid found himself hoping that a miracle would occur and Mark would change into what Dovid felt was a more normal boy.

Eight-year-old Abby, on the other hand, was both fascinated and terrified of the used bike. She went into the basement and gingerly touched the handlebars.

If only I could ride and feel the wind on my face, she thought. *But I could fall and get hurt. I don't know if I can keep my balance without someone else holding me up. I don't think I'm strong enough to keep the bike straight.*

Dovid encouraged Abby to try by offering to teach her to ride. He ran up and down the street holding onto the seat as she pedaled, constantly looking back at him to be sure that he was still holding her up.

"Okay, now Ab, you're doing great. I'm going to let go," Dovid said.

"No, Daddy. Don't let go. Please. I'm scared I'll fall," Abby screamed in terror. Then the bike teetered and Dovid had to hold it straight. Finally, without giving Abby warning, Dovid let go. At first, Abby didn't realize that Dovid had taken his hand off of the seat and she was riding alone. But once she saw Dovid was not running beside her, Abby panicked. She lost her balance and fell, skinning her knee and both elbows. Tears of accusation filled her face.

"Why did you let go, Daddy? I wasn't ready and you let me go."

"I'm sorry, Abby. I wanted you to be able to ride on your own and the only way was to let you ride without knowing that I was no longer holding on."

"I don't trust you anymore," she said, folding her arms across her chest and walking into the house.

Now the bike sat completely abandoned in the basement. Dovid was disappointed that the children didn't enjoy the bicycle but he also felt a nagging guilt for tricking his daughter. He'd had her best interest at heart, he thought she would realize that she was riding on her own and it would make her happy, but it hadn't turned out that way. He was sorry for what he'd done and worried that Abby might take a long time to forgive him. She was polite to him but he could feel that he'd lost her trust and it grieved him.

Children's feelings can be so delicate. I am not sure how to be a good father. I think I am doing the right thing only to find I am doing it all wrong, Dovid thought. *I never really had the opportunity to be a child for very long. In the Jewish religion, a boy is a man at thirteen. But, in reality a thirteen-year-old is still a child. I was a tender thirteen-year-old boy when the Nazis came. Then, between the war and the murder of my family, my childhood was stomped out. I never had the chance to play. I was busy hiding from the Nazis and then fighting on the Eastern front. I was just a child with a gun. It is only by God's miracle that I am still alive. God has been good to me even if I grew up fast. He blessed me with Eidel and my children. And I know there must be a reason that I lived while so many others perished. I only hope that someday I will know what God wants from me and why I survived. I pray that I am able to fulfill whatever it is that I have been put here to do.*

Dovid Levi was forty-FOUR years old. His hair was turning gray, there were deep lines at the corners of his eyes when he smiled. In the forty-FOUR-years he'd been on earth, Dovid had been both a wealthy man and a poor man. He had fought in a war, seen death as close as his own hand. He still carried a painful gaping hole of loss in his heart for every loved one he'd had to say goodbye to. Dovid had felt both tremendous agony and extreme joy. He would never forget the horrors beyond human imagining he'd witnessed when he liberated the camps. But he would also never forget the ecstasy he'd felt the first time he made love to Eidel, the love of his life. And then God, in his generosity, had bestowed upon both him and Eidel the joy of three wonderful, healthy children. Although Dovid was no longer a rich business owner and now only a custodian, he found himself thanking God every day for all of his blessings. Working at the temple, he learned more then he'd ever known about Judaism, and although he knew he would never be religious, he found comfort and acceptance in the comradery of being around other Jews. At the synagogue, he knew that no one would ever call him a dirty Jew. He found he liked feeling like he was a part of something bigger than himself. He'd searched for this for years but he had to be out of work and desperate to find it. Many nights someone at the temple was having a minyan, a service for the dead, for a lost loved one. In order to conduct a minyan, the rabbi needed ten men. Eidel's job was to get on the phone and call members until she got a commitment from ten men to attend the minyan that night. However, whenever they were short a man, Dovid would always volunteer to stand in.

CHAPTER FORTY-SEVEN

September 1973

For the first time since he was a boy living in his father's house, Dovid celebrated Rosh Hashanah, the Jewish New Year, and Yom Kippur, the day of atonement. He still wasn't religious, he didn't keep the dietary laws, and he wasn't keen on the structure of religion. But he loved Rabbi MIttleman, and he loved the other members of the shul, so for the first time, he wanted to celebrate the holidays. He wanted his family, especially the children, to feel like they were a part of a community. Dovid couldn't afford to send Mark to Hebrew school or give him a bar mitzvah. When the rabbi asked Dovid about sending Mark to Hebrew school, Dovid answered, "As you know we don't have the money for Hebrew school, or to give him a big fancy party like all of his friends are having. I wish I did. I would do it for him."

"Don't worry. I will see to it that he gets a good Jewish education. And there will be a party too. We will have the party right here at our Shul. The Congregation will take care of the cost."

"I couldn't allow you to do that," Dovid said.

"But that's what we do. We take care of each other. We're Jews!"

"You're too kind to me, Rabbi."

"Nonsense. When Mark is thirteen and he has finished his Jewish education, he will make a fine addition to our Jewish family of congregants. And it will bring me great naches to attend the party that welcomes him into Jewish manhood."

It was an Indian summer that year. The sun was still hot even after the Jewish New Year ended. By then it was well into September. One warm night, Dovid made hamburgers for dinner on a used barbeque grill that one of the other members of the congregation had given him. The family gathered around the table. The school year had only recently begun. The children were talking to each other about their new classmates and teachers as they were gobbling up their hamburgers. Dovid watched Eidel as she poured lemonade into glasses. Looking at her, he was suddenly struck again by how much he loved her and he felt a deep tenderness for her. The feeling was so strong that he wanted to stand up and take her into his arms. But he didn't. He was afraid that such a random display of unexplained affection might in some way frighten the children. Instead, Dovid carefully gazed into the faces of his wife and each of his children. He smiled to himself. They were so American. Every one of them looked well fed and healthy. Sometimes, he still felt a pang of sadness when he let himself think of all the money he'd once had and lost, but not right then. At that moment in time, as he was looking at his loved ones, he said a silent prayer of thanks. A tear formed in the corner of his eye, but no one noticed it. Eidel was busy going back and forth to the kitchen. The children needed this or she'd forgotten that. Mark and Haley were engaged in conversation. Abby was sulking as usual but Dovid didn't think it was anything serious. He just attributed it to the fact that she was a female. Over the years, he'd decided that women, by nature, could be moody.

That doesn't make me love my girls any less, he thought. Suddenly, Dovid felt that he was standing outside of his body and watching them as a family sitting at the table. A smile spread from his eyes to his lips.

What a beautiful family I have. I am truly blessed.

The Levis were finishing their dinner as the golden sun was setting in the west. Mark stood up, claiming he had to leave the table and go to his room to do his homework. Abby followed her brother without a word and she went to the room she shared with Haley. Haley stood up and began to help Eidel clear the table while Dovid went outside to clean the grill. There was a knock at the door. Eidel dried her hands on her apron and went to see who was there.

"Who is it?" Dovid called from the backyard.

"I think you'd better come in and see for yourself," Eidel said.

CHAPTER FORTY-EIGHT

Dovid laid the grill brush down on the ground next to the grill and walked into the house through the back door. Then he wiped his hands on a dishtowel and went to see who was waiting at the front door. Dovid put his hand to his heart when he saw who had come to visit. It was Cool Breeze. A little older, slightly thinner, and maybe a little worn, but it was him. He was alive and he was there.

Cool Breeze has come home, Dovid thought.

"Cool Breeze! Come in, come in ..." Dovid said, throwing his arms around his old friend as Cool Breeze entered. Dovid looked down at his feet and saw that Cool Breeze had a dog with him, a black lab who sat quietly

"Mister Dovi. I sure did miss you."

The two men embraced again, Dovid patting Cool Breeze's back, feeling the tears form behind his eyes. They were like lost brothers.

"Where the hell have you been?" Dovid asked.

"Here and there. I got myself into a little trouble with the law. Hell, let's us not waste time talking about this stuff. It ain't important. I got somebody I wants you to meet. This here is Buddy," Cool Breeze said, pointing to the dog. "Say hello to my friends, Buddy." The dog barked.

As soon as the children saw the dog they came running over to pet her. The dog responded by wildly wagging her tail with excitement. Buddy was affectionate with all of the children, licking them and rubbing her head against them. However, when everyone sat down in the living room, Buddy chose to put her head in Abby's lap.

Eidel went into the kitchen and put a pot of water up to boil for coffee while in the living room the two men began to reminisce. After the children went to bed, Dovid told Cool Breeze all that had happened since they'd last seen each other. He explained how he'd lost the tavern.

"Things got rough here for a while. But now Eidel and I both work at the synagogue. We're lucky to have found jobs. It wasn't easy."

"Oh, Mister Dovi, I sure is sorry to hear that. You bein' the kinda man you is, you sure don't deserve that."

"Well, it's over now. We are doing all right. I want you to know that you are always welcome to stay here," Dovid said. "But I am afraid that I don't have any spare money to pay you to do any work for me."

"I don't want no money from you, Mister Dovi. I heard tell that a new hospital just opened up here in Skokie. I am gonna see if I can get me a job there. Ifin' I can I is gonna help you and Eidel by payin' some rent. You always been a good friend to me. Now it be my turn. I'll do what I can for you now."

"Well, your apartment is still open. We haven't changed a thing down there. Except that I bought a bicycle for Mark but he didn't want to ride it so it's stored in the corner downstairs. You'll see it. It's up against the wall, shouldn't really get in your way."

"Won't nothin' get in my way. Don't you worry about that."

"I'm so glad you're here, Breeze. You had me worried."

"Thank you for lettin' me stay."

"Welcome back home. It's damn good to have you back," Dovid said.

"And Mister Dovi … I can't thank you enough for what you done for Glory. I mean the burial and all. I's truly sorry that I couldn't be there. You see, I was all balled up inside. Still is, I suppose. I loved that gal. I sure enough did." He shook his head and shrugged his shoulders. "Shouldn't a ended that way for me and her. It wasn't right how it all happened."

"I know, Cool Breeze. I know. We all felt terrible about it."

"Yeah. It sure been one long hard ride since she been gone."

"Go get some rest, my friend. We can talk more in the morning," Dovid said.

CHAPTER FORTY-NINE

The new hospital, Skokie Valley Hospital, was located on Gross Point Road, several miles from the Levi's house.

Cool Breeze got up the following morning and took a shower. Then he borrowed a clean white shirt from Dovid.

"Where you going?" Dovid asked.

"I tol you. The hospital. I be applying for some kinda job."

Cool Breeze smiled that big smile that had a way of making Dovid feel as if all was right with the world. Then Breeze winked, waved to Eidel, and walked out the door.

"Cool Breeze, don't you want something to eat?" Eidel opened the door and called after him.

"Naw, don' you be troubling yourself about me. I'll get me somethin' later."

CHAPTER FIFTY

Cool Breeze was hired by the hospital to work the three to eleven shift in housekeeping. It was minimum wage, but because he lived with the Levis it would suffice. At first, Dovid didn't want to take money for rent from Cool Breeze, but Cool Breeze insisted.

"You ain't got no money no more either," he said in his street philosopher way. "You needs this money much as I do."

Dovid nodded. "You're right. We do need it. And since we have a little extra now, we can try to do what we can to help Harry and Ida. They're having a hard time making ends meet too. The restaurant is barely paying the bills."

"Well, we gonna help them as well then."

Abby had taken to Buddy from the moment she saw him. She was a loner who trusted no one, but the dog won her heart. Buddy gladly reciprocated with the unconditional love that only an animal can give. Buddy slept on Abby's bed, and during the day she followed Abby from room to room, making it clear that she loved Abby the best of anyone in the family. Cool Breeze asked Abby if she would mind walking and feeding Buddy when he was at work and she gladly accepted. It was the first time Abby had put her heart into anything.

By the time Cool Breeze got home from work, Abby and his dog were fast asleep, wrapped in each other's arms. One night he watched them for a few minutes then laughed softly and whispered to no one, "Looks like I done lost my dog to that little girl. Well, poor little Abby needs Buddy more than I does."

Mark had his own small group of friends that he spent much of his time with. On school nights after dinner, he went into his room alone. Sometimes he talked on the phone, whispering quietly but he never came out to play games or watch television with the rest of the family.

Not meaning to hurt the other children, but unable to hide it, Eidel made it obvious that Haley was her favorite. She and Haley baked and cooked together. Haley showed an interest in learning to sew and embroider, which Eidel promised to teach her as soon as she got a little older. Haley, unlike Mark or Abby, loved to have Eidel read to her. She especially enjoyed Bible stories. Because of Dovid, Eidel was careful to read only stories from the Old Testament. However, when Haley laid her head on Eidel's shoulder and listened intently to the stories that Helen had once told Eidel, Eidel was overcome with a fierce love for her daughter.

Abby saw the bond between Eidel and Haley and felt alone and left out. Had it not been for the dog, she might have run away or turned to hurting herself. She was a strange, quiet, and frightened child. Her father was always too busy for her. He made it clear that they were living from paycheck to paycheck. It seemed that there was never enough money and he was always immersed in a desperate search to find a way to keep them from starving. Her mother was around more, but she was distant. Abby wished she could believe that her mother loved her. But, in truth, Abby felt that her mother had never really wanted her. It wasn't until Cool Breeze arrived with that scrawny black mutt with its wagging tail and soft eyes that Abby knew the real meaning of love. She adored Buddy and because she did, she became best friends with Cool Breeze.

He seemed to love all the children. Once when he was on his way home from work he found a broken record player in someone's garbage can. It was a heavy, massive wooden box, but he lugged it home and tinkered with it for weeks until he fixed it. Then he gave it to Mark who was thrilled by the gift. From then on, music could be heard coming from Mark's room every day. In his spare time, Cool Breeze built Haley a dollhouse with tiny furniture. But it was Abby who was his favorite, his dearest friend. Abby hated dolls, so Cool Breeze asked her, "Why don't you be riden that bike that's downstairs?"

She shrugged.

"You ain't never rode, have ya?"

She shook her head.

"Don't know how?"

"No, I don't."

"Well, why don' I just learn ya? It ain't that hard."

"Can you ride?"

"Sure enough. And so can you."

"Cool Breeze?" Abby said, holding Buddy's shoulder. "If I tell you something you promise not to tell anyone?"

"Sure do. Go on an' tell me."

Abby hesitated. Then she pulled Buddy closer to her. "I'm afraid to learn to ride. I'm afraid I'll fall. I've always been afraid of everything, Cool Breeze. I could never go down the slide or climb the jungle gym."

He nodded. "You scared, huh? Well, that be all the more reason you gotta do it. When you scared a somethin' the only way to get past them fears is to do it. Ifn' you let em, them fears is gonna paralyze you and seal your whole life. Sunday morning, we gonna have our first bike riden' lesson."

"I don't know if I want to."

"How about we gonna give it a try? You ain't never rode no bicycle. But let me tells you this. Once you rides, you gonna feel like you's flyin.' You trusts me?"

"Yeah, I guess…"

"Then ifn' you don't likes it. We gonna stop. What do ya say?"

"Sunday morning?" Abby said.

"Yep."

"Okay…I'll try."

"Good girl. You gonna do just fine. You'll see. You gonna surprise yourself."

CHAPTER FIFTY-ONE

Abby was terrified; it took her almost an entire day to agree, but once Cool Breeze convinced her that she could trust herself to keep her balance all on her own, she finally agreed for him to let go. Her palms were wet with sweat as she held the handlebars. Her small body was trembling. Cool Breeze ran down the street, holding the seat of the bike. Abby peddled as fast as she could. Her mind was laser-focused on holding the handlebars straight.

"Okay, my girl. Here we goes ..." Cool Breeze said as he let go of the seat. And then, as Cool Breeze had promised, Abby was flying. She was doing something she'd thought she was incapable of doing. She was riding the bike, but more importantly, she was learning to trust herself and not to be trapped in her own fears.

Mark got a job delivering papers so he could purchase records, and Haley hand-sewed clothes for her dolls out of rags that Cool Breeze brought home from the hospital.

Buddy grew fat and healthy. She was closer to Abby than ever. In fact, she no longer needed a leash; she followed Abby everywhere. By the middle of the winter of 1974, Buddy bore no resemblance to the scrawny dog who had stood on the stoop outside the Levis' door less than a year earlier.

On Sunday nights, Ida and Harry invited everyone to dinner at the restaurant. There wasn't much business, so they had plenty of time to sit around the table and catch up between customers.

Spring came with the budding of flowers and tender shoots of grass popping their heads out of the defrosting soil. One morning, Dovid got up before anyone else. A cold rain had fallen the night before, leaving a light layer of frost on the trees. In the winter it would have formed ice but because it was spring it would be melted by noon, the water nourishing the new growth. He prepared a cup of coffee for himself and sat quietly gazing out the window. Buddy came trotting out of Abby's room and sat down quietly at Dovid's side, hoping for a treat. It wasn't ten minutes before Abby followed her dog. Then Buddy stood up and, for no explainable reason, the dog dashed down the stairs to Cool Breeze's room. This was unusual behavior for Buddy. Abby started to follow Buddy, but Dovid told her to stay in the living room.

"I'll go and see if everything is all right. Cool Breeze might not be dressed."

Several minutes passed. Then Dovid came upstairs. "Cool Breeze isn't here," he said.

"Did he come home from work?" Abby asked. "Maybe he had to work a double shift. He's had to do that before."

"I'll call the hospital and see if he had to pull a double," Dovid said. He picked up the phone and dialed. Every time the rotary dial moved, the sound of it sent a shiver down his spine.

Something's not right and the dog can sense it, Dovid thought. Abby sat on the sofa with Buddy beside her…waiting.

"Thank you," Dovid said to the person on the other end of the telephone. Then he placed the handset into the receiver. "The head of housekeeping said Crawford Dell left at eleven o'clock last night. They checked Cool Breeze's time card to be sure. And it is accurate, he punched out."

"Punched out?"

"Yes, they have a punch clock. He has to put a card in it when he comes in and when he leaves. That's how they know for sure that he left at eleven."

"So where is he?" Abby said, her eyes still sleepy and her long curly dark hair a disheveled mess around her head.

"I don't know, Abby. I hope he's all right."

"He has to come back home. He would never leave Buddy, right Papa?"

Dovid nodded but he wasn't sure of anything. He was worried, confused, and had no idea what to tell the children. He just hoped that Cool Breeze hadn't started shooting again.

How can I explain that kind of an addiction to my kids? Especially Abby, she's so close to Cool Breeze. Dovid hoped Cool Breeze would return later that day with some viable excuse. But he feared the worst.

Dovid was right to be nervous about Cool Breeze. Weeks passed with no word from him. Dovid called the hospital again, only to learn that Cool Breeze never returned to work again after the night he disappeared.

Abby volunteered to take over complete care of Buddy but she missed her friend Cool Breeze. She, of all of the Levis except Dovid, was the closest to him.

"I don't know why he would just leave like that? We were friends. He never even told me he was going away. I can't believe he didn't say goodbye. What could have happened to him, Daddy? " Abby asked.

Dovid shrugged his shoulders. "I don't know, sweetheart."

He hoped that something bad hadn't happened to Cool Breeze, but there had been no call from the police. There had been no reports of an unidentified body that Dovid had been made aware of. The only answer Dovid could think of was that Cool Breeze was using again. But why? Why, when things were going so well? Dovid just had no answers.

CHAPTER FIFTY-TWO

As if Arnie were watching over his friends, a miracle happened. A food critic came to review the restaurant that the Levis and Rosens owned. The critic wrote a post in the newspaper raving about Ida's apple kugel. After the article came out in the food section of the Sun-Times it was impossible to prepare enough kugel to satisfy the customers. Ida made two trays, and each day they sold out so quickly that she increased the amount to four trays. And once people tasted the kugel they wanted to try everything on the menu. So not only was the bakery hopping, but the restaurant was filling up every night as well.

The bakery take-out orders grew so quickly that the Rosens converted the front of the store to a bakery and the back remained a restaurant.

Harry asked Dovid and Eidel to come back to work at the restaurant.

"We have so many customers that we could use the help now," Harry said. "And finally, we can all live our dream. We will have our own business again."

Dovid and Eidel discussed it. Then they talked it over with the rabbi.

"Eidel and I don't want to leave you without any help. We don't know what to do," Dovid said.

"You should go and pursue your dream," the rabbi said.

"Don't worry about me. I'll hire people. This is what you and Eidel have been hoping for … praying for."

"Yes, it is."

"And if for some reason, God forbid, it doesn't work out, you are both always welcome to come back here," Rabbi Mittleman said.

Dovid and Eidel joined Ida and Harry and six months later the business was thriving. In fact, the restaurant was so popular that there was a two-week wait to get a table at "Ida's Home Cooking." The business was growing so fast that they were able to afford to expand and rent the location next door. With the landlord's permission, they knocked the wall out, doubling the size. Now not only did "Ida's" have a bakery, but there was a lunch counter complete with its own menu, including homemade soups and deli sandwiches.

The hours they put in at the restaurant were long, but the Levis and the Rosens didn't mind. After having lost everything and being poor, they were elated with the progress of the restaurant and felt like they were living the American dream. There was plenty of money for each family to buy a car. The children had new shoes whenever they needed them, and clothes that fit them properly instead of hand-me-downs from the Salvation Army stores. No one, in either family, ever went to bed hungry again. Dovid went to the grocery store where he had stolen food during his bout of poverty and paid back every cent he'd ever stolen.

But most of all, he thanked the rabbi for his kindness in taking a chance on him and Eidel when they were in desperate need, by making a generous donation to the shul. Everything would have been perfect if only Cool Breeze had not disappeared. Occasionally, Dovid took long walks alone in the late evening. He did this to sort out his thoughts. And many times his thoughts turned to Cool Breeze.

If I could only find him. If I could only share our good fortune with him. He is the only missing piece to this puzzle.

But it was not to be, at least not then.

CHAPTER FIFTY-THREE

1975

In the summer of 1975, Mark had a beautiful bar mitzvah. Dovid refused to have the party at a banquet hall or hotel. He insisted that if he was going to pay a lot of money for an affair, it was going to be paid to the temple. He wanted to be sure that it would benefit the rabbi and the congregation that had been so kind to him through his hard times. Eidel and Ida planned everything and, even though they were very busy with the restaurant, they still managed to find the time to arrange a wonderful party. As everyone gathered in the shul, Mark stood on the bima, the platform where he would read from the Torah. Eidel had tears in her eyes as she looked up at her son. He looked so handsome with his father's deep-set dark eyes. She reached for Dovid's hand. Dovid smiled at his wife, his eyes glassy with tears of pride.

Later, at the reception, Mark sat at the head table with his parents on one side and his best friend Earl Shulman on the other. The girls he'd invited from school giggled when he asked them to dance. Dovid watched his son dancing and put his arm around his wife. He was only a few years away from fifty. It had been a long time since he had been thirteen and had stood on the bima and recited his portion from the sacred Torah. A smile came over Dovid's face as he remembered his father.

Papa, you were beaming at me from the crowd on the day of my bar mitzvah. I saw the joy in your eyes. It was many years ago. But that much I do remember. Are you here with us tonight, Papa? Is Mama here too? Tonight, your grandson, your namesake, has become a man in the Jewish religion. And just look at him Papa, he is so handsome. When I look at him, I see you in his face, in his eyes, Papa. And I know how much you would have loved him. You too, Mama. I watch him dance and talk to his friends and I wonder what his future will be. Will he be a doctor like you, Papa? I hope so. I brought him here to America where he would have the opportunity to make choices. Here he could decide what he wanted to do, what he wanted to be. I didn't have that luxury as a boy. You sent me away to save my life. And I am forever grateful. Because if you hadn't Mark, Abby, and Haley would not be here. But I will never forget the Nazis in their uniforms with their swastikas who shot you both dead for no reason at all. They knew nothing about you. They had no idea that you had a son who loved you both, or that you, Papa, were a kind and generous doctor. Or that Mama made the best chicken soup in all of Kiev and when anyone in the neighborhood was sick, she brought them a pot. You called it Jewish medicine, Papa. If I close my eyes and try hard enough I can still taste the rich broth, the perfectly textured matzo balls. Ida's soup is very good, but it's not yours, Mama. Nothing has ever been as special as yours. I believe that I can feel both of you here tonight and I know you are proud of our boy. I only wish you could be here in the flesh with us. I wish you could share your wisdom with Mark ...

"Dovi?" Eidel squeezed his hand. "Are you falling asleep?"

"No, I was just reminiscing about my parents."

"Your eyes were closed, and I was concerned. Are you feeling all right?"

"Yes, I'm fine. I feel blessed. We are, you know? We have a

fine family, good health, and now even prosperity again. Who would have thought that would ever happen? Our lives are so much better than the lives of our parents, they should rest in peace, and with God's help our children's futures will be even better than we could ever imagine."

"Mazel tov!" Harry said, as he and Ida walked over to the table. "So your son is a man tonight. You should be proud, Dovi."

"I am so very proud."

CHAPTER FIFTY-FOUR

The restaurant was open six days, Sunday through Friday. It closed early on Friday night and remained closed all day Saturday in observance of the Sabbath. Although Dovid had worked on plenty of Friday nights and Saturdays, he was enjoying the Jewish law of observing the Sabbath. It forced the family to take a day off and spend time together. Dovid even went to shul on Saturday mornings. And most Saturdays, the rest of the family accompanied him.

Early on a Saturday morning in the winter of 1976, the phone rang at the Levi house. Abby answered it. She had just gotten back from walking Buddy and was in the kitchen giving the dog a treat while everyone else was still getting ready for temple.

"Papa," she screamed. "Papa, come quick."

Dovid heard the panic in Abby's voice and came running to the kitchen with his shirt unbuttoned. "What is it?"

"It's the police. They've found Cool Breeze's body. He's dead. They want you to come and identify him." Abby handed the phone to her father. Her body was trembling.

"Oh no..." Dovid said as he took the phone. He felt his palm sweating against the receiver.

Abby stared at her father wide-eyed as he spoke to the caller, giving short answers.

"Yes." Pause. "No." Pause. "Yes." "Yes."

"Yes," Dovid said again. Then a few minutes passed. "I'll be right over there."

Dovid sank into a chair. "Eidel," he called out. "Eidel, come here."

"Be there in a minute."

"Eidel, I need to speak to you now."

Eidel came into the kitchen fastening a strand of pearls around her neck. "What is it?" she said, looking from Dovid to Abby then back to Dovid again.

"You two look like you've seen a ghost. What's going on?"

"I have to go down to the city morgue. They think that they have Cool Breeze's body."

She looked at him in disbelief. "Oh, Dovi..." She cleared her throat. "Would you like me to go with you?"

"No," he said, shaking his head as if he couldn't believe the news either.

"Maybe you should ask Harry?"

Dovid shook his head.

"Take me with you, Papa. I want to go."

It was Abby.

"I don't think it's a good idea."

"Please, Papa. I was closest to him. Buddy was his dog, now she's mine. Take me..."

"You're just a child. I'm going to the morgue. This could be very traumatic for you."

"Take me with you, Papa."

Dovid looked down at the floor. Then he looked up at Abby. "Go and get your coat."

CHAPTER FIFTY-FIVE

Dovid's heart sunk when the coroner removed the sheet from the dead body. There was no denying it. It was Cool Breeze.

"Is this Crawford B. Dell?" A police officer standing at the coroner's side asked Dovid.

"Yes," Dovid said in a small voice.

Abby was trembling.

"The only thing that Mr. Dell had in possession was this envelope in his pocket with his full name, next to your name and phone number written on it, Mr. Levi. It says right here that in case Mr. Dell is found dead, you are to be given this letter." The policeman pointed to the crude writing on the envelope.

Cool Breeze had someone write this for him, Dovid thought, holding the paper in his hand and feeling chilled.

"Can I please have a few minutes alone with his body? I would like to have a chance to read this and then say goodbye," Dovid asked.

"Sure. Why don't I take your little girl out of the room and keep an eye on her for a while so you can do what you have to do?" the officer said.

"Thank you."

Abby looked frightened as the policeman led her away. "It's okay, Abby. Go with him. I'll be right there."

Once Dovid was alone, he opened the envelope. The penmanship was poor, hard to read, but Dovid began.

"If you be readin' this Mister Dovi, it mean that I be gone on to greener pastures. I had to ask one a the men's here at the shelter to write this fer me, but it all be my words, cause I tol' him exactly what I want him to write. And, I tol him don't change nothin' I says. I know how you hates when I calls you Mister Dovi. You thinks it makes me feels like a slave. But it don't. I always calls you that outta respect, because outta everybody I ever knowd you was my true friend. And you earned my respect every day I knowd you. You stood by me no matter what kinda trouble I be getting' myself into. And that's why I'm writtin' this. Because you be deservin' some kinda explaining as to why I left your house that night that I didn't come back home after work. I left you all cause I was shamed. I be messed up on the needle again. I know how this gonna sound but truth be I can't even say how it happened. And I sure do knows that there aint never any good reason for startin' up again. Hell, I musta gone on and off the junk a hundred times in my life. The only time I actually believed I mighta been able to stay straight fer good was when Glory and me be together. After she gone, nothin' was never the same. I'd be off the stuff for a month or two then back on. I gets caught stealin' so as I can get me some more junk and I ends up in prison. I comes out straight, but for too long, I's usin' again. Don't make no sense. I knows it. Well, sure ain't no use goin' on about it now. I just be writin' this so as I can say thanks to you for bein' a real true friend in my life. And you oughta know that I likes your kids a lot. They be good kids. I sees a lot of you in them, Mister Dovi, and that sure should be makin' you feel proud. I want's to take a minute to tell you what I sees in your kids. Specially Abby. She gots a

215

heart big as Texas, but she be timid. She gots fears of life. You be her Papa, it be up to you to show her she strong enough to do whatever she want to in her future. Abby be needen this so badly so as she can grow into the strong woman I knows she can be. Now, this be important, don' you forget to tell her that she needs to take care a that dog. Although I gots to say, I already knows she gonna care for my pup. Buddy love Abby from the first time they seen each other. And Buddy sure be one good mutt. Now, Haley, she your pretty one, just like her Mama. The two of them is best friends. She gonna be all right. She always gonna be close to Mrs. Eidel, and that gonna be the way it is with her for her whole life. They like two peas in a pod. Now, as far as Mark is concerned, you gots a big problem with Mark. And you gonna find out that either you gotta love him as he is Dovi or you gonna lose him. You might not want to admit it, but you knows what I mean. You knows it deep inside your own self. Your boy, he got a lot to offer, he sure 'nough do. He be smart, and got talent too. But he also be different than the other boys. And he be different from you, Dovi. Remember my words as Mark come up and if you smart and you wants him to feel like your son, you gonna have to accept him for bein' just who he is. Well that's all I got to say. See you when your time is up, Mister Dovi. Maybe then it's gonna be the right time for us and we gonna build another juke joint in heaven, all of us, Arnie, you, Harry and me. All of us together."

Dovid folded the paper carefully as if it were a treasure and held it to his heart. Then he uncovered the body and looked into Cool Breeze's closed eyes. "If I didn't know better, I'd think you were asleep."

Dovid gave a harsh laugh. "Cool Breeze. Why my oldest and dearest friend. Why the hell couldn't you have tried

216

harder? You should have been able to fight it. Why Breeze? Why?" Dovid was yelling, his face was crimson with anger and covered with tears. "You son of a bitch. You were such a smart man. Damn it all to hell. I can't stand to see the waste of a life with so much potential. I felt like you were my brother. I trusted you and I believed in you. In fact, you might have been the only person in this entire fucking world with the courage to tell me the truth about everything, even if you knew it would hurt me or anger me." Dovid let his head fall on Cool Breeze's chest. He felt the body already beginning to grow stiff and cold. Dovid shook his head. "Rest in peace. I'm really going to miss you and your crazy wisdom." Dovid touched Cool Breeze's cheek, then he covered him with the blanket and left the room.

Tears still flowed freely down Dovi's face as he walked into the office. Abby was waiting, sitting on a bench. She looked so small wearing the dress she had planned to wear to temple that morning.

"Papa?" she said. "You're crying."

Dovid nodded. "He was very close to me. Life just won't be the same without him."

Abby got up and took Dovid's hand. They began to walk towards the car, side by side. "I just finished reading his letter. In it, Cool Breeze said to tell you that he liked you, Abby. He said you were very special to him and he is glad that you're taking care of Buddy."

That night, when everyone was fast asleep and the house was quiet, Dovid walked outside into his backyard and looked at the stars.

"Nu, old friend?" he whispered, shaking his head. "I know

you're up there. You damn fool. I can't tell you how much I wish you could have quit the needle. But even though you didn't and it finally took you away from us, I forgive you. But I have to admit that I am going to miss you every day. Who the hell is going to keep me on my toes now that you're gone? Well, Breeze, I have to say that it was a great privilege to know you. It certainly was, Mr. Crawford B. Dell. I learned so much from you. Arnie, he should rest in peace, always called you our street philosopher. And as I grew to know you over the years, I learned exactly what he meant. You had a way of looking at things and seeing them clearly, more clearly than most people. You made me laugh even when I wanted to cry, you shared my good times and bad. I'll never forget you. Never, my friend. And when I look up at the stars I'll know that you and Arnie are up there together just waiting for me to tend bar at our little slice of heaven."

CHAPTER FIFTY-SIX

Dovid purchased the plot next to Glory for Cool Breeze. They closed the restaurant for the morning to have the funeral and then the Levis and the Rosens, including Mark, Haley, Abby, and Buddy, drove to the cemetery. Dovid gave a short speech.

After the burial, everyone went back to open the restaurant. They wanted to make a dedication to Cool Breeze at the restaurant before they took the children home. Dovid parked right in front because they left Buddy in the car.

"Do you think Buddy will be okay in there, Daddy?"

"Yes. We shouldn't be long," Dovid said. Then he turned to the kids. "After you have something to eat your mother will take the three of you home. Abby, did you leave the car window open for the dog?"

"Of course, Daddy. But just a crack. I don't want her to jump out."

"Good girl."

They walked inside. Dovid carried a picture that he had framed. It was an old photo of Harry, himself, Arnie, and Cool Breeze. They were all smiling broadly, arms around each other, standing in front of the bar in the tavern. They were frozen there in the photograph. Frozen in time, all of them young, healthy, alive, together... it was so beautiful to Dovid that it hurt. And it felt like it had taken place so many years ago.

"A memorial to a good friend," Harry said, patting Dovid's shoulder.

"Yes. It's actually a memorial to all of us, but especially to our two good friends who aren't here anymore, Arnie and Cool Breeze," Dovid answered.

Just then a group of four customers came to the door. They knocked.

Harry walked over to the door.

"Are you open?" one of the men asked.

Harry looked over at Dovi and made a questioning gesture with his hands.

Dovid nodded.

"Yes, we're open, come in." Harry unlocked the door.

Two couples, about the same age as the Levis and Rosens, entered.

"Four?" Dovid asked, picking up four menus and smiling at the customers.

"Yes, four."

"Where would you like to sit?"

"The booth over there, okay?" the man gestured.

"Sure," Dovid said.

"Would you mind turning on the television?"

"Of course. Any particular channel?"

There was a television in the back of the room. Before the restaurant got busy, Ida and Harry kept it on all the time. But since the increase in business, it had not been on in a while.

Dovid turned it on.

"The news. We want to see what's happening with that Collin's bastard."

"Who's that?" Dovid was curious.

"The Nazi who wants to bring an American Nazi Party here to Skokie to march. He's trying to get a permit to bring a band of bastard, sons of bitches in full Nazi uniforms, swastikas, and everything here...right here to Skokie."

"What?" Harry said, turning the volume higher so he could hear.

"This Frank Collin has the batsum, the balls, to carry an American flag while he hangs a swastika at his meetings."

"My God," Ida said, sinking into a chair.

Dovid and Eidel sat down too.

Dovid looked for the children. He wasn't sure he wanted them to hear what the reporters had to say. At least not until he heard it first.

Abby, Mark, and Haley were sitting at a booth at the front of the restaurant eating pastries and talking amongst themselves.

CHAPTER FIFTY-SEVEN

It was true! And the worst part of it was that the American Nazis were being defended by Jewish lawyers who worked with the American Civil Liberties Union (ACLU). They were adamant about defending freedom of speech.

Dovid leaned forward in his chair and caught Harry's gaze. Harry had gone pale and so had Ida. A deep wrinkle had formed in Harry's brow. Eidel looked over at Dovid. He nodded to her and gave her a brief sad smile, as if to say, "Don't worry, everything will be all right." But she doubted that he felt that way. She folded and unfolded her napkin several times. There were tears in her eyes.

"My God," Eidel said, taking Ida's hand. "This is horrible."

"My worst nightmare," Ida shook her head.

On the television screen, Nazis in uniform were speaking. A young man named Frank Collin said they wanted to come to Skokie because Skokie had the largest population of Holocaust survivors.

"They are coming here to remind us that we are never safe," Harry said. "They want us to know that Hitler might be dead, but there are still plenty of anti-Semites in the world."

"They'll never get a permit," Dovid said.

"And if they do?" Harry asked.

"What can we do?" Ida said.

"We can always move to Israel," Eidel said. "Dovi and I were there, it's beautiful and we have a dual citizenship automatically because we're Jewish."

"Run? Not me. Not this time. I'm an old man. I've looked evil in the eye before. I know what hell is. This time, I'm not going willingly. This time they'll have to kill me. But … mind you, that won't be an easy task because I will fight until my last breath. I will do it in honor of those who I loved who died under that uniform." Harry said

"Let's hope it doesn't come to that," Eidel said.

"I hope it does. I would like to see Harry kill them. I would," Ida said. "You don't really understand. You weren't there, Eidel. They murdered my sister. For no reason, killed a young beautiful girl with her whole life ahead of her. My sister, my twin."

Eidel was trembling as she folded the napkin.

Dovid pulled Eidel's chair closer to his. Then he put his arm around her. "They will not march here in Skokie. They will not march where my wife and children have made our home."

"But Dovi, what can you do?" Eidel whispered as tears ran down her face.

"I will do whatever I have to do, my love. Whatever I have to do."

CHAPTER FIFTY-EIGHT

For a year, the American Nazi Party worked toward getting a permit to march. They argued under the guise of free speech, while the survivors openly told the press that there would be violence if they came.

"If they come to Skokie, I can guarantee you that there will be bloodshed," Rabbi Mittleman said when he was interviewed by the press.

"The entire purpose of this march is to cause us emotional pain," another survivor said on television one night.

One night, in May of 1978, Harry was so upset that he was taken by ambulance to the hospital with chest pains. Ida called Dovid and Eidel. They met her at Skokie Valley Hospital where she was waiting outside his examining room in the ER.

Harry had been having trouble breathing for hours before he finally fell, gasping for air.

"I think he is having a heart attack from all of this," Ida said. "It's too much for him."

Dovid was sick with worry. His heart was heavy with the loss of Arnie and Cool Breeze. Now he was distraught. He couldn't bear to lose Harry too.

Eidel and Ida sat together alone in the corner, while Dovid paced the room. Eidel held her friend's hand, but neither spoke.

It took several hours, but a doctor finally came out to speak to Ida.

"Your husband suffered a mild heart attack," the doctor said. "But he will be okay. He is getting on in age and the daily pressures of life are getting to him. Perhaps he should try to lighten his workload."

Ida glared at the handsome young physician.

"What do you know?" she said, her voice harsh with bitterness. "It's not the restaurant or hard work that has upset him so. Did you not see the tattoo on his arm? He's a concentration camp survivor. And I am sure you've heard the news. Such a terrible thing ... an American Nazi party. We travel thousands of miles to get away from them and they are here ... here in America. This is what has upset my husband."

"My father is a survivor," the doctor said. "He's very upset as well. So I do understand."

"Now the people on the news are saying we should ignore them. If we ignore them, they'll go away. They didn't go away in Europe when we paid them no attention. They got stronger." Ida said

"I know. It's a dilemma. The press is saying that if they march and nobody shows up that they will feel that their movement is futile and give it up."

"Eh, you think so?" Ida said, shaking her head. "I know better ... from experience. When can I see my Harry?"

"You can go in now. But he needs to stay here a few days, and I would greatly appreciate it if you would try not to upset him. Let him relax and heal."

Ida nodded. "Then take away his television set because this

stuff with the Nazis is on the TV every day."

"I think that's a good idea. Why don't you bring him some books or magazines?"

Ida nodded. The doctor walked away. Then Ida turned to Eidel. Ida suddenly looked as if she'd aged ten years during the past twelve months. Her face was lined, gray had started filtering in at her temples, and she was pale and tired looking.

"First my parents, then my sister, now my husband. Hitler is dead, but I am still not free of him."

CHAPTER FIFTY-NINE

Harry was released a week later on bed rest. He and Ida purposely avoided discussing the march. But when Dovid came to visit and the women went into the kitchen, Harry sat up in bed and looked Dovid square in the eye.

"So, are they coming?"

"Who?"

"Dovid, don't act like an idiot."

"They have been denied the permit to demonstrate here."

"That's good. Very good. But you look like you're hiding something. What is it Dovi?"

"They got a permit to march in Marquette Park. It's far away from here."

"Still, this gives them a chance to build their group. It's no good for us," Harry said. "No good at all. I want to go and show them that we aren't going to allow them to take over without a fight. Not this time. I want to gather a group and go to Marquette Park. Let's show them we are not cowards."

"Harry, you've been sick. You can't go out and fight."

"I can and I will. When is this meeting of theirs' supposed to take place?"

"June."

"You know the date?"

"Yeah, I know it. It's in ten days. But you're still so weak, Harry."

"Don't you worry about me. Go to the shul. Gather as many men as you can who are willing to go and take care of this situation."

"Okay, Harry, I will. But I don't think we should tell our wives our plans. Ida would understand. She's tough but Eidel is delicate. We both know how she can become depressed. It's best that the men involved all keep this top secret"

"I agree with you," Harry said. "And I know that plenty of the men, the rabbi included, will want to go and show the Nazis that we will never again go like lambs to the slaughter. Our slogan must be "Never Again.""

"Yes, Harry. You're right. I'll take care of it all this afternoon. For now, please try to stay calm and get better. If you don't, you won't have the strength to go with us."

"I will find the strength. If FDR could run the country from a wheelchair, I can fight with a broken heart."

Dovid nodded. He was worried that the event would be too strenuous for Harry. But he would keep his promise and organize a group of angry survivors who were eager to make Collin and his men pay for what they'd lost.

CHAPTER SIXTY

Dovid kept his promise to Harry. He talked to all of the concentration camp survivors he knew. They, in turn, talked to others that they knew. Finally, a gang of men gathered together to make plans. They were well past middle age but willing to be arrested, go to jail, or even lose their lives, if need be, in order to stop the Nazi party from growing. They knew that the march was to take place on June 25th. It was not to be in Skokie, that much they had won, but the Nazis were still being allowed to gather, to speak, and to build their party. The survivors would not tolerate this without a fight. There was a secret meeting the night before. Dovid never told Eidel where he and Harry were going but he was sure she had an idea. At the meeting, it was decided that the survivors would meet at the designated spot the following day. When Dovid arrived home, Eidel was awake. She was sitting on the sofa with the television on. He knew she'd been watching the news.

"They are going to do the demonstration tomorrow," she said. "But you already know this, I am sure."

"Yes, I know. But you shouldn't be watching it on television. You get upset easily. Everything is fine. They aren't coming here to Skokie. And that is what matters."

"Are you going to the march, Dovid?"

"Eidel," he said, walking over to her and touching her hair. "Please get some rest." He didn't want to lie to her, but he knew how easily she could become depressed.

"Are you going, Dovi?"

He looked down at the thick shag carpet, then he met her eyes. "Yes, Eidel, I have to go."

"But you could get hurt, or worse."

"I know. I know."

"What will happen to the children? How will I manage without you?"

"I will be all right."

"Dovid, please don't go."

"I love you, Eidel, but I have to go."

Dovid went into the girls' room to kiss them goodnight. Haley looked like an angel with her hair spread across her pillow. Dovid gently placed a kiss on her forehead. Buddy and Abby were cuddled together, like brother and sister. When Dovid kissed Abby, Buddy looked up at him. Then he walked into Mark's room. Mark slept soundly with the moonlight shimmering through the opening in his window shade. Dovid touched his son's cheek. Then he left the room and, as he did, he wondered whether this would be the last night he ever kissed them as they slept.

Will I return tomorrow, or will I die defending an ideal?

Dovid went back into the living room and sat down. He wanted time alone to think. Eidel was not there so he thought she'd gone to bed.

I have to leave her a note. I have to tell her where to find the insurance policies. Somehow I have to make her understand that Harry and I must do this.

He had talked to Ida the week before and Ida had promised him that if anything happened she would help Eidel raise the children.

My Eidel is so delicate and everything is hard for her to cope with. I wish I didn't have to put her through this. My God, what is a man if he doesn't stand up for what he believes in?

Eidel came out of the bedroom and walked into the living room. She sat down beside her husband and took his hand.

"Why don't we just take a break from watching the news tonight?" she said, taking his hand. "I know what you are going to do, Dovi. I am not happy about it. I am terrified of losing you. But, believe it or not, I understand why you must do this. I know that in the past I have been unstable. But I will pull myself together this time and stand behind you. If I lose you, God forbid, I will take care of the children and I will tell them that their father is a hero."

Dovid had tears in his eyes. "A hero?" He shook his head. "I am no storybook hero. I am a Jew."

"Yes," she said. "Yes."

"And ... I must stand up for my people."

"Yes, we both must. We all must," Eidel said. "Now, go and take a shower. Let's go to bed and make love. I want you to hold me close tonight, Dovi."

He nodded. Then he leaned over and kissed Eidel. "You know how much I love you?" he said.

"I think I know." She smiled, her eyes welling up with tears.

Gently, he cupped her cheek and looked into her eyes. Then he got up and went to get ready for bed.

CHAPTER SIXTY-ONE

Dovid got up early to watch the sunrise. Only Buddy sat beside him, everyone else was asleep. He tiptoed into the bedrooms to see each of his children, kissing them softly so as not to wake them. He got dressed and stood over Eidel for a few minutes, watching her as she slept. The sun was just coming up, turning the sky a pale pink and purple. He marveled at how lovely she was in his eyes, even after so many years of marriage.

Perhaps she is even more beautiful now than she was when we first met, he thought, remembering the tenderness of their lovemaking the night before. She surprised him with her strength. When he'd decided to take on this mission, he'd been afraid that she would panic and need medication in order to cope. But she had held him and told him how proud she was of him.

Eidel, my darling, my love, you never stop surprising me.

Tenderly, he placed the softest of kisses on her lips. Then he went into the kitchen. There was no need to turn on the coffee percolator. It was noisy and he didn't want to risk waking anyone. He boiled some water and downed a cup of instant coffee, patted Buddy's head and walked quietly out of the house, careful to lock the door. Until the incidents with the Nazis had begun, no one in the small Chicago suburb ever locked their doors. But now, anything might happen and Dovid wanted to ensure his family would be safe.

This could be the last time I see this house, Dovid thought as he drove down the street to pick up Harry.

Harry was ready. He held a baseball bat as he stood outside waiting. Ida was beside him.

"You want a bat?" Harry asked.

Dovid nodded. "Yes. I suppose so."

"I'll be right back. I have another one. I'll go and get it." Harry went inside.

"I'm going over to your house, Dovi. I'll wait for you and Harry there with Eidel and the kids."

"Good idea. I know Eidel will be glad you came."

"I hope I am wrong. But I am afraid that there is going to be bloodshed today," Ida said. She looked old and tired in the morning light. Never, not in all the years that the two couples had been friends, had she looked like the survivor of a concentration camp in Dovid's eyes. Today she did. Ida had never made a secret of her past. She'd always been open and honest, but her strength had always hidden the scars. Yet, as Dovid hugged her goodbye, he felt her incredible strength. It was there in her flaring anger. She was furious that Nazis had come to haunt her in America, and she was consumed with rage at what the survivors were being forced to do. But behind the fury, Dovid saw the bags from lack of sleep under her eyes. And he knew that she was masking a deep fear.

Harry came outside carrying another bat. He handed it to Dovid. The cool wood felt strange in Dovid's hand.

Ida hugged Harry tightly, perhaps a little longer than usual. Then she straightened her spine, raised her chin, and smiled at Harry and Dovid.

"God be with you," she said, as they got into Dovid's car.

CHAPTER SIXTY-TWO

Ida and Eidel sat at the kitchen table with cups of coffee growing cold in front of them. The children awakened and came into the kitchen. They were not babies anymore and so it was impossible to hide the truth from them. Haley, who was the youngest, was already turning thirteen. The three of them had seen the news. They knew that the march was to take place today, and even though it was not in Skokie, their father and Harry would be attending. They'd heard the speech the previous year on television when Meir Kahane had held a rally where he said that every Jew must arm themselves with a .22 rifle.

"You want some breakfast?" Eidel asked. The three children shook their heads.

"You should eat something," Ida said.

"No, thanks," Mark said. Then the two girls echoed him. "No."

"They can't eat. I understand," Ida said to Eidel. Eidel nodded.

"Maybe you want to go out and play, take your mind off of things?"

Again the children shook their heads. Haley began to cry softly. She laid her head on Mark's shoulder. Abby petted Buddy. "Did Papa feed Buddy before he left?" she asked her mother in a small voice.

"Yes, and he let him out in the yard. But you could walk him if you want."

"No, I'd just rather sit here."

And so they sat for several hours. No one said much but they were all thinking the same thing. *Would Papa and Harry ever return? Would they ever see them alive again?*

CHAPTER SIXTY-THREE

After all the political efforts to acquire a permit on the part of Frank Collin, only twelve pitiful young men wearing Nazi uniforms showed up for the rally at Marquette Park. Behind them, they'd hung a poster of a swastika and an American flag.

When the bus of survivors arrived, Collin was standing on a podium ranting about Jews and free speech. Dovid kept his eye on the demonstrators as he walked down the stairs of the bus. It seemed to him that Collin looked like a foolish child doing an imitation of his idol, Adolf Hitler.

The survivors held their weapons high in the air. Although they were all men well over middle age, they charged forward towards the hated symbol of the swastika and ran at the men wearing the same uniform as the men who had killed their families so many years ago.

Until the survivors arrived, the Nazis had been confident that they'd won a victory in being allowed to rally. But once they saw the charging, angry, armed men, they looked at their leader. Frank Collin's face turned white with fear. He jumped down from the podium and ran as fast as he could. His gang of thugs galloped behind him. The survivors chased them until the Nazis had run too far away to be caught. Then the rabbi turned to the others and smiled.

"Nu? So, I would consider today a victory for us! They ran away like children. This is what happens when Jews are strong."

The rest of the survivors cheered.

CHAPTER SIXTY-FOUR

Buddy was the first one to hear Dovid's car as it turned the corner and began to come towards the house. She stood up and started barking.

"Papa!" Abby said. "It must be Papa and Uncle Harry."

Ida and Eidel glanced at each other, both eager but afraid of what they were about to discover. Were their loved ones all right? There was no time to think. Soon, they would all know the truth.

It was a beautiful day in June. The sun was sparkling in a cloudless, Wedgewood blue sky.

Everyone ran outside.

The car stopped and with it, so did Eidel's breath.

Then Dovid opened the door and got out of the car. Eidel fell into his arms and began to cry. Ida and Harry embraced tightly.

Dovid bent down and took all of his children into a bear hug.

"You did it, Papa. You fought against the Nazis and you made it back home. You always told us that you would do what you could to get rid of hate and prejudice. And you risked your life to do it, just like you always said you would," Haley said.

"Hate and prejudice against any race or religion is wrong.

If today teaches you anything, let it be that. Soon, your mother and I will be old and the battle to fight against hatred and intolerance will be on you three. Fight against it. Never back down," Dovid said to the children.

"Thank God you're both here, and you're both all right," Ida whispered. "Anything could have happened today."

Harry kissed her.

"But we knew that no matter what the consequences were, we had to go," Dovid said.

"Nu, so tell us what happened?" Eidel asked.

"Come, let's go inside. We'll tell you all about it. Won't we, Dovi?" Harry said.

"We certainly will…"

<u>Another Generation</u>

Book Four in the I Am Proud To Be A Jew series.

In the final book in the Eidel's Story series the children of Holocaust survivors Eidel and Dovid Levi have grown to adulthood. They each face hard trials and tribulations of their own, many of which stem from growing up as children of Holocaust survivors. Haley is a peacemaker who yearns to please even at the expense of her own happiness. Abby is an angry rebel on the road to self-destruction. And, Mark, Dovid's only son, carries a heavy burden of guilt and secrets. He wants to please his father, but he cannot. Each of the Levi children must find a way to navigate their world while accepting that the lessons they have learned from the parents, both good and bad, have shaped them into the people they are destined to become.

AUTHORS NOTE

First and foremost, I want to thank you for reading my novel and for your continued interest in my work. From time to time, I receive emails from my readers that contest the accuracy of my events. When you pick up a novel, you are entering the author's world where we sometimes take artistic license and ask you to suspend your disbelief. I always try to keep as true to history as possible; however, sometimes there are discrepancies within my novels. This happens sometimes to keep the drama of the story. Thank you for indulging me.

I always enjoy hearing from my readers. Your feelings about my work are very important to me. If you enjoyed it, please consider telling your friends or posting a short review on Amazon. Word of mouth is an author's best friend.

If you enjoyed this book, please sign up for my mailing list, and you will receive Free short stories including an USA Today award-winning novella as my gift to you!!!!! To sign up, just go to...

www.RobertaKagan.com

Many blessings to you,

Roberta

Email: roberta@robertakagan.com

Come and like my Facebook page!

https://www.facebook.com/roberta.kagan.9

Join my book club

https://www.facebook.com/groups/14942854007982927?ref=br_rs

Follow me on BookBub to receive automatic emails whenever I am offering a special price, a freebie, a giveaway, or a new release. Just click the link below, then click follow button to the right of my name. Thank you so much for your interest in my work.

https://www.bookbub.com/authors/roberta-kagan.

MORE BOOKS BY THE AUTHOR
AVAILABLE ON AMAZON

Not In America

Book One in A Jewish Family Saga

"Jews drink the blood of Christian babies. They use it for their rituals. They are evil and they consort with the devil."

These words rang out in 1928 in a small town in upstate New York when little four-year-old Evelyn Wilson went missing. A horrible witch hunt ensued that was based on a terrible folk tale known as the blood libel.

Follow the Schatzman's as their son is accused of the most horrific crime imaginable. This accusation destroys their family and sends their mother and sister on a journey home to Berlin just as the Nazi's are about to come to power.

Not in America is based on true events. However, the author has taken license in her work, creating a what if tale that could easily have been true.

They Never Saw It Coming

Book Two in A Jewish Family Saga

Goldie Schatzman is nearing forty, but she is behaving like a reckless teenager, and every day she is descending deeper into a dark web. Since her return home to Berlin, she has reconnected with her childhood friend, Leni, a free spirit who has swept Goldie into the Weimar lifestyle that is overflowing with artists and writers, but also with debauchery. Goldie had spent the last nineteen years living a dull life with a spiritless husband. And now she has been set free, completely abandoning any sense of morals she once had.

As Goldie's daughter, Alma, is coming of marriageable age, her grandparents are determined to find her a suitable match. But will Goldie's life of depravity hurt Alma's chances to find a Jewish husband from a good family?

And all the while the SA, a preclude to the Nazi SS, is gaining strength. Germany is a hotbed of political unrest. Leaving a nightclub one night, Goldie finds herself caught in the middle of a demonstration that has turned violent. She is rescued by Felix, a member of the SA, who is immediately charmed by her blonde hair and Aryan appearance. Goldie is living a lie, and her secrets are bound to catch up with her. A girl, who she'd scorned in the past, is now a proud member of the Nazi Party and still carries a deep-seated vendetta against Goldie.

On the other side of the Atlantic, Sam is thriving with the Jewish mob in Manhattan; however, he has made a terrible mistake. He has destroyed the trust of the woman he believes is his bashert. He knows he cannot live without her, and he is desperately trying to find a way to win her heart.

And Izzy, the man who Sam once called his best friend, is now his worst enemy. They are both in love with the same woman, and the competition between them could easily result in death.

Then Sam receives word that something has happened in Germany, and he must accompany his father on a journey across the ocean. He is afraid that if he leaves before his beloved accepts his proposal, he might lose her forever.

When The Dust Settled

Book Three in A Jewish Family Saga

Coming December 2020

As the world races like a runaway train toward World War 11, the Schatzman family remains divided.

In New York, prohibition has ended, and Sam's world is turned upside down. He has been earning a good living transporting illegal liquor for the Jewish mob. Now that alcohol is legal, America is celebrating. But as the liquor flows freely, the mob boss realizes he must expand his illegal interests if he is going to continue to live the lavish lifestyle he's come to know. Some of the jobs Sam is offered go against his moral character. Transporting alcohol was one thing, but threatening lives is another.

Meanwhile, across the ocean in Italy, Mussolini, a heartless dictator, runs the country with an iron fist. Those who speak out against him disappear and are never seen again. For the first time since that horrible incident in Medina, Alma is finally happy and has fallen in love with a kind and generous Italian doctor who already has a job awaiting him in Rome; however, he is not Jewish. Alma must decide whether to marry him and risk disappointing her bubbie or let him go to find a suitable Jewish match.

In Berlin, the Nazis are quickly rising to power. Flags with swastikas are appearing everywhere. And Dr. Goebbels, the minister of propaganda is openly spewing hideous lies designed to turn the German people against the Jews. Adolf

Hitler had disposed of his enemies, and the SA has been replaced by the even more terrifying SS. After the horrors they witnessed during Kristallnacht, Goldie's mother, Esther, is ready to abandon all she knows to escape the country. She begs her husband to leave Germany. But Ted refuses to leave everything that he spent his entire life working for. At what point is it too late to leave? And besides, where would they go? What would they do?

The Nazis have taken the country by the throat, and the electrifying atmosphere of the Weimar a distant memory. The period of artistic tolerance and debauchery has been replaced by a strict and cruel regime that seeks to destroy all who do not fit its ideal. Goldie's path of depravity is catching up with her, and her secrets are threatened. Will her Nazi enemies finally strike?

Book Four in A Jewish Family Saga

Coming Early 2021....

The Smallest Crack

Book One in a Holocaust Story series.

1933 Berlin, Germany

The son of a rebbe, Eli Kaetzel, and his beautiful but timid wife, Rebecca, find themselves in danger as Hitler rises to power. Eli knows that their only chance for survival may lie in the hands of Gretchen, a spirited Aryan girl. However, the forbidden and dangerous friendship between Eli and Gretchen has been a secret until now. Because, for Eli, if it is discovered that he has been keeping company with a woman other than his wife it will bring shame to him and his family. For Gretchen her friendship with a Jew is forbidden by law and could cost her, her life.

The Darkest Canyon

Book Two in a Holocaust Story series.

Nazi Germany.

Gretchen Schmidt has a secret life. She is in love with a married Jewish man. She is hiding him while his wife is posing as an Aryan woman.

Her best friend, Hilde, who unbeknownst to Gretchen is a sociopath, is working as a guard at Ravensbruck concentration camp.

If Hilde discovers Gretchen's secret, will their friendship be strong enough to keep Gretchen safe? Or will Hilde fall under the spell of the Nazis and turn her best friend over to the Gestapo?

The *Darkest Canyon* is a terrifying ride along the edge of a canyon in the dark of night.

Millions Of Pebbles

Book Three in a Holocaust Story series.

Benjamin Rabinowitz's life is shattered as he watches his wife, Lila, and his son, Moishe, leave to escape the Lodz ghetto. He is conflicted because he knows this is their best chance of survival, but he asks himself, will he ever see them again?

Ilsa Guhr has a troubled childhood, but as she comes of age, she learns that her beauty and sexuality give her the power to get what she wants. But she craves an even greater power. As the Nazis take control of Germany, she sees an opportunity to gain everything she's ever desired.

Fate will weave a web that will bring these two unlikely people into each other's lives.

Sarah and Solomon

Book Four in a Holocaust Story series

"Give me your children" -Chaim Mordechaj Rumkowski. September 1942 The Lodz Ghetto.

When Hitler's Third Reich reined with an iron fist, the head Judenrat of the Lodz ghetto decides to comply with the Nazis. He agrees to send the Jewish children off on a transport to face death.

In order to save her two young children a mother must take the ultimate risk. The night before the children are to rounded up and sent to their deaths, she helps her nine year old son and her five year old daughter escape into a war torn Europe. However, she cannot fit through the barbed wire, and so the children must go alone.

Follow Sarah and Solomon as they navigate their way through a world filled with hatred, and treachery. However, even in the darkest hour there is always a flicker of light. And these two young innocent souls will be aided by people who's lights will always shine in our memories.

All My Love, Detrick

Book One in the All My Love, Detrick series.

Book One in the All My Love, Detrick Series

Can Forbidden Love Survive in Nazi Germany?

After Germany's defeat in the First World War, she lays in ruins, falling beneath the wheel of depression and famine. And so, with a promise of restoring Germany to her rightful place as a world power, Adolf Hitler begins to rise.

Detrick, a handsome seventeen-year-old Aryan boy is reluctant to join the Nazi party because of his friendship with Jacob, who is Jewish and has been like a father figure to him. However, he learns that in order to protect the woman he loves, Jacob's daughter, he must abandon all his principles and join the Nazis. He knows the only way to survive is to live a double life. Detrick is confronted with fear every day; if he is discovered, he and those he loves will come face to face with the ultimate cruelty of the Third Reich.

Follow two families, one Jewish and one German, as they are thrust into a world of danger on the eve of the Nazis rise to power.

You Are My Sunshine

Book Two in the All My Love, Detrick series.

A child's innocence is the purest of all.

In Nazi Germany, Helga Haswell is at a crossroads. She's pregnant by a married SS officer who has since abandoned her. Left alone with the thought of raising a fatherless child, she has nowhere to turn -- until the Lebensborn steps in. They will take Helga's child when it's born and raise it as their own. Helga will now be free to live her life.

But when Helga has second thoughts, it's already too late. The papers are signed, and her claim to her child has been revoked. Her daughter belongs to Hitler now. And when Hitler's delusions of grandeur rapidly accelerate, Germany becomes involved in a two-front war against the heroic West and the fearless Russians.

Helga's child seems doomed to a life raised by the cruelest humans on Earth. But God's plan for her sends the young girl to the most unexpected people. In their warm embrace, she's given the chance for love in a world full of hate.

You Are My Sunshine is the heartfelt story of second chances. Helga Haswell may be tied to an unthinkable past, but her young daughter has the chance of a brighter future.

The Promised Land:

From Nazi Germany to Israel

Book Three in the All My Love, Detrick series.

Zofia Weiss, a Jewish woman with a painful past, stands at the dock, holding the hand of a little girl. She is about to board The SS Exodus, bound for Palestine with only her life, a dream, and a terrifying secret. As her eyes scan the crowds of people, she sees a familiar face. Her heart pounds and beads of sweat form on her forehead...

The Nazis have surrendered. Zofia survived the Holocaust, but she lives in constant fear. The one person who knows her dark secret is a sadistic SS officer with the power to destroy the life she's working so hard to rebuild. Will he ever find her and the innocent child she has sworn to protect?

To Be An Israeli

Book Four in the All My Love, Detrick series.

Elan understands what it means to be an Israeli. He's sacrificed the woman he loved, his marriage, and his life for Israel. When Israel went to war and Elan was summoned in the middle of the night, he did not hesitate to defend his country, even though he knew he might pay a terrible price. Elan is not a perfect man by any means. He can be cruel. He can be stubborn and self-righteous. But he is brave, and he loves more deeply than he will ever admit.

This is his story.

However, it is not only his story; it is also the story of the lives of the women who loved him: Katja, the girl whom he cherished but could never marry, who would haunt him forever. Janice, the spoiled American he wed to fill a void, who would keep a secret from him that would one day shatter his world. And...Nina, the beautiful Mossad agent whom Elan longed to protect but knew he never could.

To Be an Israeli spans from the beginning of the Six-Day War in 1967 through 1986 when a group of American tourists are on their way to visit their Jewish homeland.

Forever My Homeland

The Fifth and final book in the All My Love, Detrick series.

Bari Lynn has a secret. So she, a young Jewish-American girl, decides to tour Israel with her best friend and the members of their synagogue in search of answers.

Meanwhile, beneath the surface in Israel, trouble is stirring with a group of radical Islamists.

The case falls into the hands of Elan, a powerful passionate Mossad agent, trying to pick up the pieces of his shattered life. He believes nothing can break him, but in order to achieve their goals, the terrorists will go to any means to bring Elan to his knees.

Forever, My Homeland is the story of a country built on blood and determination. It is the tale of a strong and courageous people who don't have the luxury of backing down from any fight, because they live with the constant memory of the Holocaust. In the back of their minds, there is always a soft voice that whispers "Never again."

Michal's Destiny

Book One in the Michal's Destiny series.

It is 1919 in Siberia. Michal—a young, sheltered girl—has eyes for a man other than her betrothed. For a young girl growing up in a traditional Jewish settlement, an arranged marriage is a fact of life. However, destiny, it seems, has other plans for Michal. When a Cossack pogrom invades her small village, the protected life Michal has grown accustomed to and loves will crumble before her eyes. Everything she knows is gone and she is forced to leave her home and embark on a journey to Berlin with the man she thought she wanted. Michal faces love, loss, and heartache because she is harboring a secret that threatens to destroy her every attempt at happiness. But over the next fourteen tumultuous years, during the peak of the Weimar Republic, she learns she is willing to do anything to have the love she longs for and to protect her family.

However, it is now 1933. Life in Berlin is changing, especially for the Jews. Dark storm clouds are looming on the horizon. Adolf Hitler is about to become the chancellor of Germany, and that will change everything for Michal forever.

A Family Shattered

Book Two in the Michal's Destiny series.

In book two of the Michal's Destiny series, Tavvi and Michal have problems in the beginning of their relationship, but they build a life together. Each stone is laid carefully with love and mutual understanding. They now have a family with two beautiful daughters and a home full of happiness.

It is now 1938—Kristallnacht. Blood runs like a river on the streets, shattered glass covers the walkways of Jewish shop owners, and gangs of Nazi thugs charge though Berlin in a murderous rage. When Tavvi, the strong-willed Jewish carpenter, races outside, without thinking of his own welfare, to save his daughters fiancée, little does his wife Michal know that she might never hold him in her arms again. In an instant, all the stones they laid together come crashing down leaving them with nothing but the hope of finding each other again.

Watch Over My Child

Book Three in the Michal's Destiny series.

In book three of the Michal's Destiny series, after her parents are arrested by the Nazis on Kristallnacht, twelve-year-old Gilde Margolis is sent away from her home, her sister, and everyone she knows and loves.

Alone and afraid, Gilde boards a train through the Kindertransport bound for London, where she will stay with strangers. Over the next seven years as Gilde is coming of age, she learns about love, friendship, heartache, and the pain of betrayal. As the Nazis grow in power, London is thrust into a brutal war against Hitler. Severe rationing is imposed upon the British, while air raids instill terror, and bombs all but destroy the city. Against all odds, and with no knowledge of what has happened to her family in Germany, Gilde keeps a tiny flicker of hope buried deep in her heart: someday, she will be reunited with her loved ones.

Another Breath, Another Sunrise

Book Four, the final book in the Michal's Destiny series.

Now that the Reich has fallen, in this—the final book of the Michal's Destiny series—the reader follows the survivors as they find themselves searching to reconnect with those they love. However, they are no longer the people they were before the war.

While the Russian soldiers, who are angry with the German people and ready to pillage, beat, and rape, begin to invade what's left of Berlin, Lotti is alone and fears for her life.

Though Alina Margolis has broken every tradition to become a successful business woman in America, she fears what has happened to her family and loved ones across the Atlantic Ocean.

As the curtain pulls back on Gilde, a now successful actress in London, she realizes that all that glitters is not gold, and she longs to find the lost family the Nazi's had stolen from her many years ago.

This is a story of ordinary people whose lives were shattered by the terrifying ambitions of Adolf Hitler—a true madman.

And . . . Who Is The Real Mother?

Book One in the Eidel's Story series.

In the Bible, there is a story about King Solomon, who was said to be the wisest man of all time. The story goes like this:

Two women came to the king for advice. Both of them were claiming to be the mother of a child. The king took the child in his arms and said, "I see that both of you care for this child very much. So, rather than decide which of you is the real mother, I will cut the child in half and give each of you a half."

One of the women agreed to the king's decision, but the other cried out, "NO, give the child to that other woman. Don't hurt my baby."

"Ahh," said the king to the second woman who refused to cut the baby. "I will give the child to you, because the real mother would sacrifice anything for her child. She would even give her baby away to another woman if it meant sparing the baby from pain."

And so, King Solomon gave the child to his rightful mother.

The year is 1941. The place is the Warsaw Ghetto in Poland.

The ghetto is riddled with disease and starvation. Children are dying every day.

Zofia Weiss, a young mother, must find a way to save, Eidel her only child. She negotiates a deal with a man on the black market to smuggle Eidel out in the middle of the night and deliver her to Helen, a Polish woman who is a good friend of Zofia's. It is the ultimate sacrifice because there is a good chance that Zofia will die without ever seeing her precious child again.

Helen has a life of her own, a husband and a son. She takes Eidel to live with her family even though she and those she loves will face terrible danger every day. Helen will be forced to do unimaginable things to protect all that she holds dear. And as Eidel grows up in Helen's warm maternal embrace, Helen finds that she has come to love the little girl with all her heart.

So, when Zofia returns to claim her child, and King Solomon is not available to be consulted, it is the reader who must decide...

Who is the real mother?

Secrets Revealed

Book Two in the Eidel's Story series.

Hitler has surrendered. The Nazi flags, which once hung throughout the city striking terror in the hearts of Polish citizens, have been torn down. It seems that Warsaw should be rejoicing in its newly found freedom, but Warsaw is not free. Instead, it is occupied by the Soviet Union, held tight in Stalin's iron grip. Communist soldiers, in uniform, now control the city. Where once people feared the dreaded swastika, now they tremble at the sight of the hammer and sickle. It is a treacherous time. And in the midst of all this danger, Ela Dobinski, a girl with a secret that could change her life, is coming of age.

New Life, New Land

Book Three in the Eidel's Story series.

When Jewish Holocaust survivors Eidel and Dovid Levi arrive in the United States, they believe that their struggles are finally over. Both have suffered greatly under the Nazi reign and are ready to leave the past behind. They arrive in this new and different land filled with optimism for their future. However, acclimating into a new way of life can be challenging for immigrants. And, not only are they immigrants but they are Jewish. Although Jews are not being murdered in the United States, as they were under Hitler in Europe, the Levi's will learn that America is not without anti-Semitism. Still, they go forth, with unfathomable courage. In New Life, New Land, this young couple will face the trials and tribulations of becoming Americans and building a home for themselves and their children that will follow them.

Another Generation

Book Four in the Eidel's Story series.

In the final book in the Eidel's Story series the children of Holocaust survivors Eidel and Dovid Levi have grown to adulthood. They each face hard trials and tribulations of their own, many of which stem from growing up as children of Holocaust survivors. Haley is a peacemaker who yearns to please even at the expense of her own happiness. Abby is an angry rebel on the road to self-destruction. And, Mark, Dovid's only son, carries a heavy burden of guilt and secrets. He wants to please his father, but he cannot. Each of the Levi children must find a way to navigate their world while accepting that the lessons they have learned from the parents, both good and bad, have shaped them into the people they are destined to become.

The Wrath Of Eden

The Wrath of Eden Book One.

Deep in them Appalachian hills, far from the main roads where the citified people come and go, lies a harsh world where a man's character is all he can rightly claim as his own. This here is a land of deep, dark coal mines, where a miner ain't certain when he ventures into the belly of the mountain whether he will ever see daylight again. To this very day, they still tell tales of the Robin Hood-like outlaw Pretty Boy Floyd, even though there ain't no such thing as a thousand dollar bill no more From this beautiful yet dangerous country where folks is folks comes a story as old as time itself; a tale of good and evil, of right and wrong, and of a troubled man who walked a perilous path on his journey back to God.

The Wrath of Eden begins in 1917, in the fictitious town of Mudwater Creek, West Virginia. Mudwater lies deep in mining country in the Appalachian Mountains. Here, the eldest son of a snake-handling preacher, Cyrus Hunt, is emotionally broken by what he believes is his father's favoritism toward his brother, Aiden. Cyrus is so hurt by what he believes is his father's lack of love for him that he runs away from home to seek his fortune. Not only will he fight in the Great War, but he will return to America and then ramble around the United States for several years, right through the great depression. While on his journey, Cyrus will encounter a multitude of colorful characters and from each he will learn more about himself. This is a tale of good and evil, of brother against brother, of the intricate web of family, and of love lost and found again.

The Angels Song

The Wrath of Eden Book Two.

Cyrus Hunt returns home to the Appalachian Mountains after years of traveling. He has learned a great deal about himself from his journey, and he realizes that the time has come to make peace with his brother and his past. When he arrives in the small town where he grew up, he finds that he has a granddaughter that he never knew existed, and she is almost the same age as his daughter. The two girls grow up as close as sisters. But one is more beautiful than a star-filled night sky, while the other has a physical condition that keeps her from spreading her wings and discovering her own self-worth. As the girls grow into women, the love they have for each other is constantly tested by sibling rivalry, codependency, and betrayals. Are these two descendents of Cyrus Hunt destined to repeat their father's mistakes? Or will they rise above their human weakness and inadequacies and honor the bonds of blood and family that unite them?

One Last Hope

A Voyage to Escape Nazi Germany

Formerly *The Voyage*

Inspired by True Events

On May 13, 1939, five strangers boarded the MS St. Louis. Promised a future of safety away from Nazi Germany and Hitler's Third Reich, unbeknownst to them they were about to embark upon a voyage built on secrets, lies, and treachery. Sacrifice, love, life, and death hung in the balance as each fought against fate, but the voyage was just the beginning.

A Flicker Of Light

Hitler's Master Plan.

The year is 1943

The forests of Munich are crawling with danger during the rule of the Third Reich, but in order to save the life of her unborn child, Petra Jorgenson must escape from the Lebensborn Institute. She is alone, seven months pregnant, and penniless. Avoiding the watchful eyes of the armed guards in the overhead tower, she waits until the dead of night and then climbs under the flesh-shredding barbed wire surrounding the Institute. At the risk of being captured and murdered, she runs headlong into the terrifying, desolate woods. Even during one of the darkest periods in the history of mankind, when horrific acts of cruelty become commonplace and Germany seemed to have gone crazy under the direction of a madman, unexpected heroes come to light. And although there are those who would try to destroy true love, it will prevail. Here in this lost land ruled by human monsters, Petra will learn that even when one faces what appears to be the end of the world, if one looks hard enough, one will find that there is always A Flicker of Light.

The Heart Of A Gypsy

If you liked Inglorious Basterds, Pulp Fiction, and Django Unchained, you'll love The Heart of a Gypsy!

During the Nazi occupation, bands of freedom fighters

roamed the forests of Eastern Europe. They hid while waging their own private war against Hitler's tyrannical and murderous reign. Among these Resistance fighters were several groups of Romany people (Gypsies).

The Heart of a Gypsy is a spellbinding love story. It is a tale of a man with remarkable courage and the woman who loved him more than life itself. This historical novel is filled with romance and spiced with the beauty of the Gypsy culture.

Within these pages lies a tale of a people who would rather die than surrender their freedom. Come, enter into a little-known world where only a few have traveled before . . . the world of the Romany.

If you enjoy romance, secret magical traditions, and riveting action you will love The Heart of a Gypsy.

Please be forewarned that this book contains explicit scenes of a sexual nature.

Made in the USA
Monee, IL
04 November 2022

17113292R00152